MOONSHAKER

MOONSHAKER

G V CHILLINGSWORTH

Order this book online at www.trafford.com
or email orders@trafford.com

Most Trafford titles are also available at major online book retailers.

Printed in the United States of America.

ISBN: 978-1-4669-0635-8 (sc)
ISBN: 978-1-4669-0634-1 (hc)
ISBN: 978-1-4669-0636-5 (ebk)

Library of Congress Control Number: 2011961940

Trafford rev. 08/25/2012

www.trafford.com

North America & international
toll-free: 1 888 232 4444 (USA & Canada)
phone: 250 383 6864 ♦ fax: 812 355 4082

To my team of hard-working and dedicated proofreaders: Debbie, Emma, Adam, and Scott. Without your help, this book may not have had as many words.

PROLOGUE

N ews bulletin talking about an asteroid striking the Moon:
"Scientists at the Hawaiian observatory have confirmed that a meteor will strike the Moon in four days' time."

News bulletin five days later:
"These amazing pictures show the moment the meteor actually struck the Moon. Notice the dust cloud that was thrown into space, which gives the appearance, from the Earth, that the Moon is egg shaped."

Six months later:
"In breaking news—scientists have verified that the Moon has been knocked out of its orbit and is actually moving closer to Earth.

With more on this story, we cross to James Wilson and with him is a spokesman of the Earth Observatory. Are you there James?"

"I'm here Terry, and with me is Dr Anthony Rush. Dr Rush, you say the Moon is moving towards the Earth, but how quickly is it moving?"

"It is not like it is hurtling towards the Earth, James. It is actually moving closer at approximately 600 millimetres per year."

"Now, Dr Rush, to me, that does not sound like a lot. Why should we be so concerned?"

"It may not seem like a lot, James, but as it gets closer to Earth, its gravitational pull will start to have a devastating effect."

"How so, Dr?"

"As we know, the Moon's pull creates the tides, and the closer it gets, the stronger that pull would be. Only trouble is, when it gets too close, you could well have something like a 100-metre tide, travelling around the world twice a day. Also, the pull on the tectonic plates would start to increase volcanic activity, as well as tropical storms increasing in magnitude by a factor of three."

"Sounds like that could be a bit of a problem."

"Yes, James, it does."

*   *   *

Twelve months later, in a large boardroom seated around a conference table a group of people were discussing the problem.

The man who stood to explain his plan to rectify the situation to the group was Dr Raul Western, and even though he was not someone who embraced sport—or, as he would prefer to think of it, running against a stopwatch—he was a man with a rather athletic build.

If asked about this, he would simply say that it was a combination of hard work and a sensible diet, ideals that his parents had instilled in him from an early age.

Speaking in front of a large group of people who did not have a background in science made him feel a little anxious, but nevertheless, he knew that his idea was viable.

"Although the satellite that needs to be built would far outsize anything attempted before," he said, "it would need to be this size, so that the impulse gun could be carried into space and then operated from a solid base.

"Then, once in position at a predetermined distance from the Moon, we would fire the impulse gun, which would then in turn send shockwaves towards the Moon.

"Once we have the setting needed to give us enough power in the shockwave to attain our objective, it would then be a matter of just firing until the Moon is gently nudged back into its orbit."

"So, this thing can be done?" asked General William Fredrickson, commander in chief of the world alliance of armed forces.

Even though he had been in the army just over forty years, he thought that maybe this project would be his last. The question he asked was not really a question requiring an answer as much as a statement requiring confirmation.

"With sufficient manpower and facilities, yes it can be done," Western replied with conviction he hoped to be believed.

"Dr Western, if we were to give you access to a certain military facilities and ensure that you had hands on deck, what time frame are we talking about?"

"Well, General," Western replied courteously—even though he was not a man with a military background, he still knew enough to know that to not show respect to high-ranking military officer would be very disrespectful, and he needed all the help he could get with this project and pissing people off would not get it—"I think the best-case scenario would be three years, but realistically, it would be operational in five."

"Well then, it sounds to me as though we have a plan. I will have some people get in contact with you, and we'll get started."

And with that, the project was up and running.

As the meeting appeared to be breaking up, Dr Western collected his papers and headed out the door, when he heard a voice behind him.

"Dr Western, how does it feel to be the saviour of Earth?"

When he turned around, he saw the question was asked by James Rodrigess, the spokesman for the United World Council, who was in direct contact with the League of Seven.

Though he was not of large stature, Rodrigess gave the appearance of someone who had an aura of confidence about themselves and who made you feel confident in their ability to achieve what it was that they set out to achieve,

"We are not there yet, Mr Rodrigess."

"You underestimate yourself, Dr Western."

"No, I just find that if you try to get too far ahead of yourself, it is difficult to go back if something goes awry."

"I am sure, Dr Western, that with your skills, the military's help, and the support of the World Council, things that go awry will be few and far between."

"Thank you for your optimism, Mr Rodrigess. I will try not to disappoint you."

"I am sure you won't, Dr Western. I am sure you won't."

"Excuse me, sir."

The voice was from a tall thin man who gave the appearance of someone who had forgotten what the sun looked like several years ago, as the whiteness of his complexion seemed to glow under the room's lights.

"Dr Western, may I introduce Peter Hicks, the head of our PR division. He is the one setting up the press conference."

"Press conference, already? But we have only just finished discussing it. Shouldn't we wait until we have a more comprehensive idea of what we are doing?" was the slightly stunned response from Dr Western.

"Dr Western, I know the scientist in you wants to dissect and re-examine every little detail over and over again before you start a committee to discuss your findings, but you know this thing is going to happen and I assume you have a plan on how it is going to happen, so now what we have to do is let the public know so that we can start to garner their support."

"Why would people not support this project?" responded Dr Western, "I mean, if we do not do this, they know the only outcome is catastrophe on a global scale."

Mr Rodrigess sighed before answering, "Unfortunately, Dr Western, there are people out there who think this is the way it should be. I mean, there are some that think the culling of the human race would be a good thing, and then there is the Anti-Interference League.

"Now, I am not saying that we give them every little detail, but let them know that we are not sitting on our hands on this issue and dispel any rumours or suspicions that people may have, and believe me, the more public support that we have, the easier this thing will flow."

YENDOR

"Overbeing Blet, it is a great moment in our time to know that with your leadership we are to cross the great void of space in the knowledge that we will insure the continuation of the mighty Yaglot race."

The statement came from Commandling Zaldark, a well-respected leader of the military forces.

The commandling struck rather an imposing figure, for even though he was over two metres tall, a height not overly impressive for a Yendorian, he had the broadest shoulders that Blet had seen for some time, and Blet knew that it was from many cycles of hard work in battle and training that had created them.

Also, over the course of time the leathery Yendorian skin became thicker and darker, but he would be hard pressed to find someone with skin as dark as Zaldark's.

"Your great fullness is welcomed, Commandling Zaldark. It shows keenness that you wish this mission to be a success," said Blet

"The furthering of the Yaglots through time and space is all that I have ever wanted," replied Zaldark.

"Then let us all move towards that goal, Commandling."

"Overbeing Blet, may I speak with you a moment?"

The request came from Chief Advisor Rerkr, and although he was not overly short, standing just less than two metres tall, the fact that Overbeing Blet was two and a half metres in height, tall even by Yendorian standards, meant that Rerkr had to strain his neck back when in close proximity, to be able to talk to him.

"Excuse me, Commandling Zaldark. It seems I am needed elsewhere."

"Of course, Overbeing, I look forward to our departure."

As Blet watched the commandling walk away, he turned to his advisor and asked, "Are we sure that Zaldark is the correct one for this mission?"

"Of course, sir. Protocol was followed, and Commandling Zaldark was by far the most obvious choice," replied Rerkr. "Why do you ask?"

"It just seems to me that he may be thinking that he is getting ready for a major battle," Blet answered.

"I assure you, sir, that he is the one who all the troops look to for leadership. He has a great strategic mind, and as you do not know what you may encounter on your voyage, we cannot see the sense in leaving anything to chance. As a superior once told me, if you are looking at it, you are not looking for it," said Rerkr.

"That is good, but what does that have to do with this mission?" Blet then asked.

"It means, sir, that if you need someone in a crisis, he will be there."

"Well, hopefully, I will not need to look for him."

"That is what we all hope, sir."

"Now, Adviser Rerkr, what was it that you needed to speak to me about?" Blet asked with little attempt to hide his impatience.

"It is about the importance of this mission, Overbeing," Rerkr said with his head slightly bowed.

"Every Yaglot knows the importance of this mission," was the terse response.

"My apologies, Overbeing," Rerkr quickly replied, "it was not my intention to try and tell you something that was well known by all, but there is something that no one has been told for the sake of absolute security."

"Go on."

"When the elders were first told of this mission, they realized immediately its importance, and on further discussions, they have come to a decision that you are to be accompanied by some of their number."

After a few seconds, to let the gravity of this statement sink in, Blet replied, "This is indeed of some significance. When am I to be informed of the details?"

"You are to be summoned to the grand hall in one rotation at mid time [noon]," said Rerkr, with a feeling of some importance again.

"Thank you, Rerkr. I shall be ready."

HOME

W hilst at the checkout of the supermarket that he stopped at on his way home that evening, Dr Western looked at a hollo-screen that was playing a news broadcast about the planet-shifter program.

On it, the presenter introduced a spokesperson for the Anti-Interference League.

"Mr Rogerson, why is it your organization feels so strongly against this program?"

"Well, Terry, as well you know, we at the league believe that everything that happens does so for a reason, and that reason, no matter how oblivious we are to it, is God's work and we have no right to try to alter it."

"Even if it means death and destruction on a massive scale?" asked the presenter next.

"If that is what God wants, Terry, then who are we to question him?"

"Some would say though, Mr Rogerson, that the reason we make these decisions is because God gave us the ability to choose to do so."

"Some might also say so, Terry, but because children have the ability to play with guns, should they then be allowed to?"

"So, Mr Rogerson, are you saying that we all are no more than children?"

"In the presence of God, Terry, I am saying we are less."

"Thirteen credits please," came the voice of the counter clerk, taking Western's attention away from the images floating just above the clerk.

"Sorry, here you are," he said, handing the clerk his identity card.

"Dr Western, I saw you on the news bulletin earlier today. I think it is brilliant what you are going to do. Too bad about those nut jobs from the Anti-Interference League."

"Oh, is that a professional assessment?" inquired Dr Western with a wry smile on his face.

"No, it's just that you are going to do what you are doing because, if we do nothing, the whole world is in trouble, and those people at the League are only interested in their own agenda," was the clerk's impassioned response.

"That is as may be," said Dr Western, "but even nut jobs have a right to their own opinion."

"Well, in my opinion, they should all be used as fuel for your rockets; then they will finally be a help to humanity."

"Seems a little extreme, but I think we are going to be all right for fuel anyway," was Dr Western's attempt at a diplomatic reply.

"Thank you for your custom, Dr Western. Here is your card and receipt. Have a wonderful evening."

"Thank you," was Dr Western's reply as he gathered his groceries and headed out to his car.

*   *   *

As Dr Western pulled into his driveway, he noticed his daughter peering out of the window of the living room, and he could not suppress a smile that spread across his face.

As he entered his house, the first thing he saw was his daughter, jumping up and down excitedly and exclaiming, "Dad! Dad! Dad! I saw you on hollo-vision today, and Tania said that I could call Tracy and Leah."

Tania was the name of his current wife and Ellie's step mother. His first wife, Ellie's birth mother, had been killed in a car accident nine years earlier.

Tracy and Leah were her classmates.

"Really? How did I look? Was I the mostest handsomest man ever?" he asked, as he picked her up, whilst the smile on his face seemed to be growing bigger and bigger with every passing moment.

"Well, nearly as handsome as Frederick Peers Varn," was the reply.

High praise indeed, as Frederick Peers Varn was the latest singing/ acting sensation to almost every English speaking pre-teen on the planet.

As his wife entered the room, she explained that Ellie was just so engrossed when she saw his press conference, and that she could not wait to call her friends.

After he had put Ellie down and Dr Western and Tania were putting away the groceries, Tania said, "I saw that horrid Graeme Rogerson in an interview, just before you got back."

"Yes, I saw it at the supermarket," he replied.

"Why won't he just mind his own business and stop trying to enforce his ideals on others?" said Tania, with more than a little annoyance in her voice.

"Sounds like you should be speaking to Trevor at the supermarket."

"Why do you say that?" asked Tania.

"It is just that he said the same thing," explained Dr Western.

"Yes, well obviously a lot of people think the same way," his wife said.

"And I will say the same thing that I said to Trevor," said Dr Western, "and that is, that everyone is entitled to their own opinion."

"Leah says that her dad said that a rabbit did a poo in Mr Rogerson's head, and now he can't think properly." said Ellie, trying to contribute to the conversation.

"Even if someone did say that, it does not mean that you should repeat it. You know better than that Ellie," said Dr Western, with what he hoped was a stern look on his face.

"Yes, Dad," was the sorrowful reply.

"When can I go and see the space ship you are building, Dad?" was Ellie's next, not so subtle, conversation-changing question.

"It is not a space ship, Sweetie. It's a satellite that is going to put the Moon back where it belongs."

"What are you going to do with it after you put the Moon back?" was Ellie's next question.

"Well, after that, it will be used as a space station for experiments. It is not going to be ready for a couple of years yet, but when it is, I promise that I will take you," Dr Western replied, seeing the excitement in Ellie's eyes.

"Butterfly promise?" asked Ellie, holding up her right arm, with her fingers extended towards her father.

Holding up his own arm and extending his wiggling fingers until they just touched the tips of Ellie's fingers, he said, "Butterfly promise," and he knew that was one promise he could not break.

GRAND HALL

As Blet entered the hall, he could not help but feel the presence of all the sayers who had passed through the building before.

This may have been helped by the fact that the walls were covered in the carvings of the sayers throughout the ages.

"Overbeing Blet."

Blet turned to see Rerkr coming out of the door leading to the inner sanctum, which was a place that very few Yaglots got to go.

As Blet walked through the door for the second time—the first being when he was honoured with the title, overbeing—he was struck, as he was the first time, with an almost overwhelming sense of awe and tradition, for on the other side of the room was the council of sayers. And, even though they could not be thought of as young, the sayers had a presence about them that made them seem larger than life itself.

They were dressed in the finest flowing garments that could only be created by master craftsmen. They were seated in their large, ornately carved chairs behind a magnificent table carved in one piece from a huge Bandagar tree, which was said to have fallen in a storm, thus allowing many Yaglots, including members of the first council of sayers, to use it to cross a ravine and escape to higher ground and therefore avoid being swept away in a massive flash flood.

Many think it was the Great Protector that made the tree fall, and therefore, the desk should always be.

"Overbeing Blet, we are honoured by your presence."

The statement came from Elder Bnotkl.

"The honour is mine alone, Respected One," was Blet's subservient reply.

"Please, let us be a little less formal, and hopefully this meeting will be more productive," said Bnotkl.

"As you wish," was the only reply that Blet could give.

"Overbeing Blet," this time it was Elder Ciotkr speaking, "we have asked you here, because we feel that we have made a decision that you should be told of before we tell others."

"That, of course, is your decision to make," said Blet, with lowered eyes, knowing that the sayers did not need, nor would ever ask, for his permission.

"It is, but as it does impact on you, we thought it right that you be the first to be told," said Ciotkr.

Blet did not reply but just waited for the explanation he knew was forthcoming.

"Overbeing Blet, we chose you for this mission because we knew you had the authority, respect, and knowledge to bring about a successful conclusion," explained Ciotkr. "As everyone knows, our star is dying, and that is why we are looking to new colonies, but what no one else knows is that, according to our knowledge seekers, the dying star is going to have a severe effect on the sky hole."

"May I ask what that effect might be?" asked Blet.

"Of course," said Ciotkr. "They are telling us that as the star deteriorates the impulse field that gives the skyhole its stability is somewhat weakened, and the number of passages that we will be able to take through it are going to be reduced significantly."

"Will we still be able to send the full number of ships through to start the new colony?" asked Blet, sensing that he already knew the answer.

Bnotkl was the one to answer.

"As we cannot be sure when the skyhole will become too unstable, we have agreed that your journey will be one that cannot return."

Blet was trying to comprehend what he was just told and formulate questions that would help him understand when Bnotkl explained further.

"As you will not be returning, you will now be taking the newest design skyships, allowing you to take three times the number of citizens and supplies, thus allowing you to be able to set up the new colony much more easily. Then, if we are able, we will send more ships through until the skyhole becomes too unstable."

"What will happen to those that are left behind?" asked Blet, feeling numb at the thought that countless numbers of his fellow citizens, would be left to perish on a doomed planet.

Ciotkr replied, "The knowledge seekers are searching the skies and have already located three possible sites for new colonies."

"Also," added Bnotkl, "the skyship builders have already created new plans for even bigger ships so that we will be able to transfer as many citizens as we possibly can. The disadvantage is that without a skyhole, it will take many cycles to reach them and then return.

"Then, once we have established the new colony, we shall seek out your colony, but again, because this will take many cycles [430 days per cycle], it has been decided that three of our number are to accompany you so that when you arrive there will be a council."

"It has also been decided," continued Bnotkl, "that as well as taking your core group, that is, both sharebeings and three younglings, you shall be able to take twenty others of your choosing."

"Do we know when we are to begin our journey?" asked Blet.

This time, the question was answered by Elder Aletrot.

"The time that has been set for your departure is one half of one cycle from this time."

"How easily will I be able to locate a suitable area for the new colony?" was Blet's next question.

"Several sites have already been located by the surveillance ship, and the crew will be able to relay this information to you, once you come out of the skyhole," explained Aletrot.

"How long after we leave the skyhole will we arrive at the new colony?" asked Blet, knowing that to ask too many questions at this meeting would be counterproductive as he would not be able to remember every detail and to ask the same question again at a later date would harm the perception that others had of him as a strong minded and confident leader of the people.

"That will take eighteen rotations," said Aletrot.

"Then, if that is what is to be done, I can do no more than to be ready for when that time comes," replied Blet.

"Thank you for your time, Overbeing Blet," said Ciotkr. "I look forward to our next meeting."

"I am at your call as always," said Blet with a slight bow before turning to leave, as he knew the meeting was over.

Once back in the Grand Hall, Blet saw Rerkr waiting.

As Blet approached, Rerkr said, "The sayers have told me to assure you that you will be the first to be told of any further decisions they make pertaining to the mission."

"Let them know that I thank them for the honour of being taken into their confidence and that I eagerly await their instructions," was Blet's reply, before leaving the Grand Hall and heading back to his official residence to inform his family about and start preparing for their epic journey.

T minus 10-9-8

Four years, seven months, and twelve days later.

As he was dropped at his house by Corporal Raymand, the driver who had been assigned to him when the project started, Dr Western noticed the house had very few lights on.

He checked his watch only to find that it was just past midnight, and that was probably a good indicator as to why.

"Good night, or should I say, good morning, Ian? I shall see you at nine," he said to his driver.

"I shall see you at nine, Dr Western," said Ian, still not referring to him by his first name after almost five years.

Once inside, Western noticed Tania asleep in the armchair, her reading glasses on her chin and a book on her chest.

On the hollo-vision screen a weatherman was saying that the current bad weather should clear up for next Thursday's launch.

As he turned the screen off, he heard a weary voice behind him say, "Hey, I was watching that."

He looked at his wife and said, "Yes, I could see you were totally engrossed."

"I thought that they might let you rest before you take off next week," said Tania, reaching up to hug her husband.

"I could have been home hours ago, but we had a little problem," he said, starting to feel a little weary himself.

"How little?" asked Tania.

"The Anti-Interference League tried to smuggle someone onto the base, and after he was found out, there was a full security check," he explained.

"So, if they are still trying to stop you, how secure is the project? I mean, is it still going to be safe to launch?" asked Tania becoming very much awake now and with a slight look of concern on her face

"Actually, they may have done us a favour by trying what they did," said Dr Western.

"How so?" asked Tania, now with a look of curiosity on her face.

"The fact that they are still trying to sabotage the project at such a late stage tells us that they have not been successful in implementing any earlier plan. It also shows us that the security measures that are in place are more than effective, and therefore, in answer to your question, the project is still secure and it is going to be very safe to launch," said Dr Western, hoping that his wife would see it the same way and relax enough so that they could go to bed.

"OK, but I would still be a lot happier if Graeme Rogerson was in prison," said Tania, making no attempt to hide the contempt that she felt towards Rogerson.

"Well, they can't charge him for today's excursion, because as he always says, the organization denounces the use of violence and the individual, although he admires his commitment, acted on his own behalf," explained Dr Western, now really looking forward to a hot shower and a nice warm bed.

"That really shows the calibre of the man, when he won't even admit to what he is doing," said Tania, working herself up even further.

"Look, don't worry about him or his organization. They are not going to stop or damage the project, it is going to go smoothly, everything will work perfectly, and when I alone have singlehandedly and successfully completed the mission, I shall return as the greatest superhero in the history of all time," said Dr Western, striking what he thought to be a heroic pose.

"If that is the case, then why are the others going?" asked Tania, with a cheeky grin returning to her face.

"Well, obviously, to make my coffee," he said, "because you know how much we superheroes like our caffeine."

"All right Mr Superhero, maybe it is time we both got some sleep," said Tania.

"That sounds like a wonderful idea," he said. "My superheroing will just have to wait."

"I am glad to hear it," said Tania, again hugging her husband.

"Speaking of superheroing, how is Ellie?" Dr Western asked.

"She is a teenager, so of course she is going to be upset that you spend so much time at work and so little time with her," Tania's responded.

"OK," he said with a sigh, "I shall talk to her at breakfast."

"I think a little reassurance from you would be a good thing for her," said Tania, turning to head up the stairs to go to bed.

"It may not do me much harm either," said Dr Western, following closely behind.

* * *

The next morning, as Dr Western and Tania were sitting at the kitchen table, Ellie walked in with a look of absolute disinterest in anything on her face.

"Good morning, Sweetie," said Dr Western, knowing that a positive start was a good start.

"Morning," came the unenthusiastic, mumbled reply.

"How are things at school?" was his next question, which he thought could possibly lead into an in-depth conversation, whereby everyone's problems could be talked over and solved in a trice.

"Good," was the less than conversation-inspiring reply.

"Anything exciting planned?" he asked, hoping to elicit more than a one-word response.

"Noooo," was the elongated response from Ellie, who gave a look of someone that had just been asked if she wanted to eat some mud.

"OK," said Dr Western, soldiering on. "How are you going with your judo?" thinking that he had gotten onto a subject that would excite her.

"I'm going to quit," said Ellie, staring at the table with a dour look on her face.

"What? But why? I thought you really liked it," was Dr Western's stunned reply.

"What does it matter? You don't really care anyway," said Ellie, snatching up her school bag and heading for the door.

"Ellie," said Dr Western, hoping his daughter would stop and talk to him.

"I have to go. Terry is picking me up at the corner," said Ellie, as she continued on her way out the door.

"What—?" was the only response he could muster, whilst at the same time looking at his wife in shocked disbelief as to what had just happened.

"As I said. She is a teenager, and she is angry at the fact that you are paying more attention to others than you are to her," said Tania.

"But, if I don't do this—"

"I know," said Tania before he could finish, "but she feels as though you have been ignoring her since this project started, and she is at an age when she really needs her father, even if it is just to argue with him."

"So, you are saying that the only time I am going to be able to speak to her is when she wants to yell at me?"

"Pretty much," said Tania.

"Something to look forward to," he said, pondering how to deal with the situation.

"You know, she is still upset at the fact that you broke your promise to her about showing her the project," said Tania, trying to show one of the reasons why she may be unhappy.

"Oh, man, I did, too, didn't I?" he said, rubbing his forehead with the fingers on his right hand. "It is just that I was so busy trying to stay on schedule that I lost focus on her."

"Well, now you are ahead of schedule, maybe you should try to do something that will help you reconnect," said Tania, hoping to plant the seed of an idea that might just blossom.

"Yeah, I will talk to the people at the base and organize it so that she can come in tomorrow," he said, still upset at the fact that he had not noticed what was happening.

"If you could, even though she may not show it, I think she will really like that," said Tania.

"OK, I will organize that first up," he said, starting to feel a little better about himself.

"And by the way, who is Terry?" he asked when he finally remembered what had been said.

"Let's tackle one thing at a time," said Tania. "Even superheroes can get overloaded."

"Oh, man," said Dr Western, now rubbing his whole face with both hands.

THE GREAT JOURNEY

As Blet was leading his core to the shuttle that would transport them to the skyship, he noticed Rerkr walking towards them.

"Overbeing Blet, may the Great Protector watch over your core," said Rerkr, knowing that to ignore Blet's family unit would be a great insult.

"Adviser Rerkr, your words are welcome," said Blet, acknowledging the sincerity in Rerkr's words.

"The sayers have asked that you accompany them to the skyship and that they may meet your sharebeings and younglings," said Rerkr.

"That will be an honour for us all," replied Blet, knowing it would also allow him to find out which of the sayers would be accompanying them on their journey. For security reasons that had been a very closely guarded secret.

"Then, if you would follow me please," said Rerkr, who proceeded to lead them away from the throng of people heading towards the shuttles and down a corridor that led to a large double door that was guarded by two very large, armed guards

"Is it necessary for weapons to be carried?" asked Blet, not really knowing what to think.

"I assure you, Overbeing," said Rerkr, "that the guards are purely for ceremonial purposes, and that there is absolutely no need for concern."

As they approached, each guard turned and opened their respective doors.

When they entered, Blet saw four more guards, standing two on each side of the three sayers that were sitting at a large desk.

"Overbeing Blet, please do not be alarmed by the guards. It is just that protocol decrees that each sayer shall have two personal guards when travelling."

The explanation came from Elder Bnotkl.

Blet turned to see that the two guards at the doors had now closed them and were inside.

"Overbeing Blet," said Elder Glerci, who was the youngest sayer ever to have been appointed, "we thought that we could spend this time with you, as we know that, once this journey begins, you will be very busy, and we would not wish to interrupt you."

"Your words are kind, Elder Glerci," said Blet, "but you would only have to say so, and my time will be yours."

"We are only three," said Elder Zotstot, the third sayer of the group, who, Blet had been told, came from a remote area on the other side of Yendor, "and we would not think of taking time away from the other citizens on the skyship, as they are just as important to this expedition as we three."

Although Blet did not fully agree that the sayers were not of more importance than the other citizens, he knew that once the sayers had said something, it was so.

"Overbeing Blet," again it was Bnotkl that spoke, "another reason we asked to see you was so you could see which of our numbers would be making this journey."

"Explanations are not necessary," said Blet. "I only need to know that your journey is a safe and comfortable one."

"Your words are kind, Overbeing Blet," said Bnotkl, "but I think we should get to know each other, at least a little, before our journey."

"I, as is well documented, am the longest-serving sayer of all councils. Elder Glerci is the youngest sayer ever. So, that between us, we have an understanding of a wide range of citizens of various ages."

"Also with us is Elder Zotstot, who, being from a very remote area of Yendor, will be very useful in helping to set up the new colony."

"Greetings to you all," said Blet. "Now if I may introduce my core, these are my sharebeings, Kretyabotkl and Etklet, and my younglings, Zcetklot, Bnerkr, and Rlckl."

"May this journey be a safe one for you all," said Elder Bnotkl, addressing the group.

"And to you," said Kretyabotkl, as she was the senior of the two sharebeings and therefore the matriarchal figure.

Blet turned to see Rerkr re-enter the room and realized that he had not notice him leave.

"The shuttle can now take us to the skyship if everyone is ready," Rerkr said, more as a statement of option rather than a suggestion.

"Then let us begin the next stage of our journey through life and see where it takes us," said Bnotkl with a smile on his face as he looked at the three younglings.

Blet saw that Bnotkl was trying to ease any tension that he thought that the younglings may have, but he could have assured him that they had done nothing but talk about this trip since they were first told of it, and for the last few rotations, it was more than he could do, to keep them calm.

"A great journey indeed," said Zotstot, "and a wondrous existence in our new home."

They all then headed to the door that would lead to the shuttle.

TIME TO GO

As Dr Western walked along with the other crew members, all in their flight suits ready for lift off, he looked over at the viewing room that was for family and dignitaries and was glad to see Ellie standing next to Tania. Although Ellie did have what could only be described as the teenager scowl, Tania had assured him that, since he organized her excursion to the project, she was a lot happier knowing that he was taking an interest in her again.

Now all he had to do was figure out the Terry situation.

But first, he thought he would tackle the easy job of pushing the Moon back into place.

The next two rooms were absolutely packed with media from all points of the globe, and this helped to drive home the fact that this was no small task.

As they walked down the corridor that led to the elevator that would take him to the command centre of the vessel, he looked out of one of the windows at what some people were calling the giant mushroom.

He could see why some called it that, because it was more domed at the top and not pointed and the impulse gun looked like a flared stem below it. However, mushrooms do not usually have five thrust rockets spaced at equal distance around their perimeter, nor were they usually twenty metres across.

A part of him was still upset that people would want to trivialize it and not call it by its correct name, the name that he actually chose: Moonshaker One.

If only everyone was a scientist, then they would understand, he thought.

"Dr Western," came a voice that brought him back to the here and now, "has everyone done their pre-board check?"

The question was asked by the pre-flight personnel safety supervisor, and although he was not sure of the title, Dr Western knew that the man's job was of the utmost importance.

One thing he did not want to happen was a major disaster that could have been avoided by a simple check.

"Yes," was the reply.

"Does everyone have their own personal equipment?"

"Yes."

"Does everyone know their role in the lift off stage?"

"Yes," he said, and although he just wanted to say, "No, oh my God, I have forgotten how to do this," just to lighten the mood, he thought better of it.

So, for the next few minutes, he just set about answering all the questions asked.

When all the questions had been asked and answered, the supervisor held his hand out to Dr Western and said, "Good luck to you Dr, and may you and your crew succeed and return safely."

Reaching out and shaking his hand, Western replied, "Thank you, Andy. We will try."

With that handshake Mission Control knew that everything was good to go.

When he turned and entered the elevator that would take him and his crew the ninety metres up to the entry hatch, Dr Western started to wonder if there was anything that could have been done differently or better. He then thought that it was probably just a little bit late to be thinking about changes now.

"Dr Western," came a voice that brought his attention back to the present moment.

The voice belonged to a very attractive, and some said brilliant, young female astrophysicist.

"Yes, Dr Anders?" Dr Western replied.

"At what level of power do you envisage that you will need from the device to obtain the required objective?"

"Well, Dr Anders," Dr Western's replied, "that is what we are going to find out."

For, even though he designed the Palentium core drive, he had only been able to gauge his findings on smaller impulse guns and computer simulations.

He did know, though, that the drive would not only give them power for thrust in space, as well as power for the planet shifter, it would also, when activated, increase its own density, thereby creating an artificial gravity. It was placed between the control room and the planet shifter so everything would seem to happen below them.

"So," he continued, "we will do a few test runs in low orbit first, with a starting point of maybe 15 to 20 per cent to gauge how well things are working without the restrictions of gravity, then a few more at a higher percentage before we move out to a close enough range to actually have an effect."

He thought that to be a well thought-out and informative response.

"Do we know how close that is going to be?"

This time the question came from Tony Watson, the chief pilot, not a man of huge stature but, still, he gave the impression of someone who did not want to fail.

Dr Western looked at him, and remembered that he had been chosen for this mission because he was the best test pilot that the air force had had. And Western knew that Watson must be brave to test fly something for the first time without knowing if it would be a total success or not, and he prayed that this would be one of those times and that he could come back and boast to everyone how well it went.

"That is probably a question best directed towards Dr Peterson, as he is our computer expert," said Dr Western.

To look at him, nothing would strike you as being out of the ordinary with Dr Peterson. If you were to see him on the street, you would just see another large, slightly overweight, middle-aged man, even though he did like to tell people that he remained fit by playing squash and having a sauna once a week with his associates. But, if you were to give him a computer and an "unsolvable" problem, he would soon be able to show you, in more than one way, why it actually was not unsolvable.

"Again," explained Dr Peterson, "as Dr Western has said, we will have to use trial-and-error methods to obtain our objective, for even though we have run countless computer simulations, nothing is going to tell us more than an actual test."

"Then let's just hope that everything works the way it should," said Tony.

"Hey, it will work, don't you worry about that," said Gary Roebottom, the engineer and co-pilot. "Some of these parts took at least a couple of seconds to throw together."

As Dr Western knew Gary's sense of humour, he was the only one that did not stare at him with a look of absolute uncertainty.

"I'm only joking," said Gary, now with a huge grin on his face. "Some of them took minutes."

The rest of them realized that they should not take Gary Roebottom too seriously.

Just then, the elevator slowed to a halt, and they all knew this was really happening.

When they had all made their way inside and were in the process of securing themselves into their allotted seats, Tony turned to the supervisor, as he had ridden up with them, and gave him the thumbs up, signifying that everything was good and the hatch could be sealed, although he did not like that term as it implied that the door could not be opened again.

He then made sure, that the door was securely latched from the inside as well, before moving to his own seat next to Gary at the controls.

Then, for the next forty-five minutes, they were just checking system after system, until finally, Mission Control said, "All systems check."

Then asked Tony, "We are go or no go for lift-off?"

Tony then asked the others, one by one, if everything was all right.

When they had all confirmed that they were all good, he replied, "Mission control, we are go for lift off."

"Thank you, Moonshaker. Commencing lift-off, in zero minus sixty seconds."

AND SO IT BEGINS

When Blet had made sure that the sayers and his core were comfortably ensconced in their quarters, he made his way to the skyship command centre.

When he arrived, he saw Controller Krerbnot speaking to a female, and as he approached, Krerbnot looked up and saw him walking towards them.

Although Krerbnot was not as tall as Blet, because of the authority he had, he had an aura about him that seemed to make him appear larger than he actually was.

"Overbeing Blet, I hope everything is satisfactory with your rooms."

"More than adequate thank you," said Blet.

"And the sayers, have they settled well?" asked Krerbnot, knowing full well that nothing was spared in trying to make their quarters as comfortable as possible.

"Yes, they are most satisfied with their lodgings," Blet replied.

"That is good," said Krerbnot.

"May I introduce Starguide Zyaot?" he continued. "She finished her sky teachings as the highest-scoring Yendorian of all time."

"Excellent work, Starguide Zyaot," said Blet. "We are indeed grateful that the Great Protector has given you the knowledge that you may be able to help us in our quest."

"I see it as my duty to be able to help in any way that I could, Overbeing," said Zyaot with a slight bow of the head and a look of eager anticipation in her young eyes.

"A worthy sentiment indeed, Starguide Zyaot," acknowledged Blet.

"Thank you, Overbeing," said Zyaot with another nod of the head.

"And this is Maintainer Zeral," said Krerbnot, introducing someone that was intent on studying data screens, and did not seem to have much of a concern for anything else.

"It is an honour to meet you, Overbeing," said Zeral, tearing himself away from his screens.

"When I was told that I had been chosen for this trip, I was truly thankful of the Great Protector, knowing that I would have the honour of making this trip with you."

"Your words are kind, Maintainer Zeral," said Blet. "Hopefully we will both enjoy this privilege."

"So, is everything working to your satisfaction Zeral?" asked Krerbnot.

"Well Controller, the new Krandon crystal propulsion unit is functioning well, and we are only two particles off having full gravity but we should have that before we reach cruising speed," replied Zeral.

"And how long will that be?" asked Krerbnot.

"We will be at cruising speed in five small time sections," answered Zeral.

"How long will it then take us to reach the skyhole?" asked Blet.

"That will take a further twenty-five rotations, time wise," said Zeral.

"Then once in the skyhole," he added, "it will be a further twelve rotations time wise before we come out of the other side, but in that time, we will have travelled a distance that would normally take over half a lifetime to cross."

"And how is it that the skyhole functions in this way?" asked Blet with genuine interest.

"Our knowledge seekers are still trying to learn its secrets, Overbeing, but at this time, they only know it as a giant swirling mass of solid light," explained Zeral.

"What do you mean by solid light?" Blet then asked.

"Although it is a just a mass of rotating light, they say the sides are somehow of such density that nothing can penetrate them," Zeral said.

"And what would happen," asked Blet, "if the sky whole should collapse whilst we are in it?"

"Then," said Zeral, looking straight at Blet with an expressionless face, "we would find ourselves in the great void of space, somewhere between here and where we want to go, and, if the Great Protector is merciful, we would be in one piece."

"Fortunately," said Krerbnot trying to lighten the mood," we have more than an ample supply of Kaldingi plant, so at least we will not go hungry."

"Ah," said Blet, "Kretyabotkl makes the most wonderful Kaldingi fruit and dried forest-serpent stew, that I have ever tasted."

"Then I shall make sure that she is able to obtain those ingredients, Overbeing," stated Krerbnot.

"And I shall consider you my guest the first time that she prepares it, Controller Krerbnot," said Blet, knowing how much he himself enjoyed it every time that dish was served.

"Then I shall look forward to the honour of dining with you and your core, Overbeing."

"As I shall look forward to your company, Controller," replied Blet.

SO THIS IS SPACE

After the initial noise and vibration and the feeling that his body was trying to escape itself, Dr Western could not help but be amazed at the serenity of his new environment. That his body felt weightless and was gently trying to float free of the restraints holding him in his seat and also that the Earth was now floating by his window, truly astonished him.

"All systems functioning normally," said Tony.

"Is everyone OK?" he then asked.

When each of them answered in the affirmative, he then said, "Good, let's get to work then."

"Well, Doc," said Gary, "let's see if this Palentium core drive of yours, really works."

Then, for the next forty-five minutes, Dr Western and Gary carried out a series of preliminary checks.

When everything was reading as it should, Gary turned to Dr Western and said, "OK, Doc, it's now or never."

All Dr Western had to do now was to type the word "activate" into the computer and he would find out if the best part of five years were wasted or not.

Slowly he typed in the word and pressed "enter".

Nothing happened.

Before he could think that it was not going to work, he saw that in his excitement and anticipation he neglected to notice the computer screen, which now had a question on it, ARE YOU SURE YOU WANT TO ACTIVATE PALENTIUM CORE, followed by a choice of either YES or NO.

He pressed YES.

Nobody said anything, and just as he was starting to think of things that could be at fault, Dr Western heard a low humming noise emanating from below the control room.

Then everyone noticed that they were being pushed back into their seats, and loose items that were tethered with short pieces of string that were floating in mid-air, were now hanging towards the floor or resting on ledges.

"Hey, Doc, I think I'm putting on weight," said Gary, finally relieving the tension.

"Yes, well thankfully, we all are," said Dr Western, in a voice full of relief.

"Dr Western, how long before we obtain one atmosphere?" asked Dr Anders.

"It should take no more than a couple of minutes, and then we will be able to move around as if we were back on Earth," he explained.

"Except," said Gary, "that when you take your dog outside for a walk, you will have a lot more room."

More than one person looked at him as if to say, "Man, how long are we up here with you?"

"Gary," said Dr Western, "I will need you to help me run the diagnostics on the core to make sure everything is all OK, before we even attempt to operate the planet shifter."

"Can do, Doc," was his short and direct answer.

"How long before we start getting a few shots away?" he then asked.

"After we have analysed all the data thus far, we should be able to start testing in about two days," came the reply, "and that should give us all plenty of time to prepare for our ultimate goal."

"What's that, to win a lifetimes supply of whiskey and cigars and a date with Miss Long Legs International?" asked Gary, which prompted even Dr Western to think this was going to be a long mission.

THE PASSAGE

As they got closer to the skyhole, Blet was awestruck as to how such an anomaly could exist.

Krerbnot, who had seen the skyhole on several occasions, was not awestruck as much as he was curious as to the apparent changes in the outer edges of the entrance to the skyhole.

Whereas before there was a definite edge, now there seemed to be more of a haze, but he told himself, doubt was a luxury he could not afford at this time and the knowledge seekers had assured him that it would be safe to pass through.

"Truly remarkable," said Blet.

"Yes," replied Krerbnot.

"I still remember the first time I travelled through it," he continued. "I was so struck by just how incredible it was that I forgot about my task at hand. Needless to say, my superior gave me quite a few extra work shifts so I would have time to realize, that a task not completed is a problem beginning. I certainly made sure that from that moment on, every task I was given was definitely completed before I started something new."

"I think that is a good ethic to have in all facets of life," said Blet, "one that I myself, try to instil in my younglings."

"Speaking of which, I am sorry they could not be here to witness our entry into the skyhole, but regulations do not allow for such things as the entry is such a precise manoeuvre there can be no distractions. You, as overbeing, are, of course, exempt from those regulations," explained Krerbnot, "and," he continued, "once we have entered the skyhole, there is no regulation prohibiting you from escorting your younglings to the command centre.

"Also," he added, "to watch as we exit the skyhole is quite spectacular, and as it is more like flying out of a tunnel than a precision manoeuvre, there is no regulation stating that they cannot watch it from here."

"Thank you, Controller Krerbnot," said Blet. "I am sure they will like that."

Just then, Maintainer Zeral said, "We are about to enter the skyhole, Controller."

"Very good, Maintainer," said Krerbnot as he reached over to the control panel to activate the ship's announcement system.

"This is Controller Krerbnot speaking," he said. "We are about to enter the skyhole, and you may feel the ship shake ever so slightly. Please do not be alarmed, as this is quite normal. Also, those with a viewing portal may wish to look out as we enter, for it is quite a spectacle and one that should not be missed. For those who are not able to witness it, we will be showing images on all personal viewing screens.

"Now, Overbeing, behold the wonder that is the skyhole," said Krerbnot, as he himself made sure to watch.

The ship did shake ever so slightly, as Krerbnot had stated it would, but anyone who was watching as they entered the skyhole would have quickly forgotten any concern that they may have had over it.

The entrance, which looked like a massive, slowly rotating electrical storm, was soon replaced by brilliant colours of every hue and shade imaginable that seemed to leap at you as you passed by. Then, they were replaced by clouds of swirling colour that were infused with what looked like a million glowing swamp beetles that danced around the ship as it made its way through them.

And, every now and then, what appeared to be lightning bolts of various colours flashed past.

"I am always amazed when I see what has just occurred," said Krerbnot. "Even more so, when I think that not even the knowledge seekers can fully explain why it is as it is."

"Thank you for allowing me to witness the event from here, Controller," said Blet. "It is not something I shall soon forget."

"I am honoured that I was able to be present the first time that you saw it, Overbeing," said Krerbnot.

"Hopefully, my younglings will find exiting the skyhole to be just as fascinating," said Blet.

"I am sure they will, Overbeing," said Krerbnot, "and I look forward to that day."

"As I am sure they will as well, Controller," said Blet.

TEST ONE . . .

Dr Western leaned forward slightly to speak into the microphone, which was not actually necessary as it was so sensitive it could pick up a whisper at ten metres.

"Mission Control, this is Moonshaker One. All systems checked and ready for test of impulse gun," he said with a hint of nervous anticipation in his voice.

"Moonshaker One, roger that. All recording systems set and ready for your first test," came the reply.

"Very good," said Dr Western, unsure of what else to say at a moment like this.

"Moonshaker One set at parallel to Earth, and the first test to be at 15 per cent."

"Firing in five, four, three, two, one."

And with that, he pressed the button on the computer screen that said "fire". Then the secondary button that asked if he wanted to fire and gave him a choice of either "yes" or "no".

He pressed "yes".

All that could be seen from inside Moonshaker One was a bright, green flash that could have rivalled the sun, only to be accompanied by an almost deafening explosion and the whole craft shuddered violently.

"Is everyone OK?" asked Dr Western, once he had regained his footing, as the violent shaking had almost made him fall.

"We're OK," said Gary, speaking for himself and Dr Peterson, who he was helping to stand up again as he had been knocked off his feet.

"Dr Anders and I are all right," said Tony.

"What in the world just happened?" asked Dr Peterson.

"I don't know, but you may want to see this," said Gary as he pointed out the window towards Earth.

As they all reached the window, they looked out just in time to see the clouds suddenly and violently disperse as a shock wave passed through them and continued towards the surface of the planet.

Once it hit, a massive cloud of dust erupted, then started to spread, like ripples in a pond from where a stone was thrown, and continued on its way around the globe.

"What the hell is that?" asked Gary.

"My best guess would be a shockwave created by the explosion," said Dr Western.

"Will it cause much damage?" asked Tony.

"Well, the circumference of the Earth, is about 40,000 kilometres, and judging by the speed that the dust cloud is spreading, I would say it will cover that journey in about five minutes," said Dr Western. "So, I think a shock wave travelling at 8,000 kilometres a minute is going to cause a considerable amount of damage."

"What? Like a massive cyclone or tornado?" asked Gary, more in hope than anything else.

"If you consider a severe cyclone or tornado to have winds of 250 kilometres an hour, then think that that this shock wave is travelling at 480 thousand kilometres an hour," Dr Western explained, like everyone else, not really wanting to believe, let alone contemplate, the outcome of this incident.

After a few moments, Dr Western said, hoping to distract the others by getting them to do the job they were sent to do, "So, I think that what we should do now is check to see if we have sustained any damage. Then, we should see if we can contact Earth."

"What do you mean, if we can contact Earth?" asked Tony.

"It is just that the shock wave has more than likely disrupted the radio communications of everyone," Dr Western explained.

"Gary, once I have checked that the readouts are all fine, I will need you to go and physically check the core."

"Dr Anders and Dr Peterson, I need you to check all the other monitoring devices, as well as your own equipment, and Tony, you can try and reach Mission Control."

After he had checked the readouts for the core, and Gary had been down to see if anything had been damaged, Dr Western was glad to see that the core had, indeed, not been damaged. When Drs Anders and Peterson both confirmed that all other systems were working normally, he started to feel a little more at ease.

Unfortunately, try as he might, Tony could not raise Mission Control.

"Could it be an external problem with the craft?" asked Dr Anders.

"If the antennas were damaged some way by the explosion, then that would stop us from being able to contact anyone," said Tony. "The only way to really check it would be to go outside and have a look."

"OK," said Gary, "I will go out and check the antennas, and whilst I am out, I will also check the impulse gun."

"While you are doing that, I may as well go on and check the rest of the ship for damage," said Tony.

"Dr Peterson," said Dr Western, "could you check all the data that we have around the time of the explosion and see if you can find any anomaly, and I will do a thorough check of the Palentium core information."

"Dr Anders," he continued," see if you are able to locate any of the outstations. Once located, we can try to contact them. If you can't locate the one near Mars, try for the one circling Ganymede. It has the more powerful receiver, and that could be our best bet."

"Do you really think that we will be able to contact them?" asked Dr Anders.

"Well, the shock wave would not have been able to travel that far, and even if it did, it would have been so weak when it arrived that it would barely register on any of their gauges let alone cause any damage."

"So, if we can send a signal, hopefully someone is listening, and, well, we've just got to try," was Western's reply.

"Gary, Tony," he said as he turned, "do not forget to use your tether lines, for even though we have gravity in the ship, if you move away from it, obviously, its effect is weakened," Dr Western explained.

"So, Gary," he continued, "if you wanted to jump back to Earth, you probably could."

"Always wanted to break the Olympic high-jump record." said Gary, with a huge grin on his face.

"You might have a bit of a problem sticking the landing though," said Dr Western. "But in all seriousness, just be careful and pay attention to what you are doing, because a mistake out here could be fatal."

"Don't worry, Doc. We'll be careful," said Gary in one of his rare serious moments.

As Gary and Tony went to suit up for their first spacewalk, Dr Western set about the task of going over his own data, to see if he could find even the minutest detail that could give them some indication as to what could have happened.

After about ten minutes, Gary's voice came over the intercom.

"Hello, can anyone hear me in there?" he asked.

"We can hear you, Gary," Dr Western replied when he finally reached the intercom.

"Well, at least we know we have local comms," said Gary.

"Yes, that is something I suppose," replied Dr Western.

"Right," said Gary. "We are both suited up, and we need you to unlock the outer door, so we can then open it to get out."

"Outer door is now unlocked," said Dr Western as he flipped the corresponding toggle switch.

Gary's voice came back. "Opening outer door now." Then, after a few seconds he said, "And man, what a view."

"OK, Gary. Focus and make sure you are tethered," said Dr Western, slightly tersely.

"Yeah, done, Doc. Just making my way to antennas now, and they don't appear to be damaged so it must be like you said that the shock wave has interfered with radio communication."

"I'm going to check on the impulse gun, so I will call you back in a minute or two," he said.

"OK, Gary, let us know what you find."

"Tony, can you hear me?" Dr Western then asked.

"Loud and clear," came the response.

"Anything untoward to report?"

"Nothing so far," said Tony. "I have checked the top and most of the side, and when I am done here, I will give Gary a hand."

"That would be good," said Dr Western, who about to turn his attention back to his own task of data checking when Gary's voice came back on the intercom.

"Doc, you there?" Gary asked.

"Here, Gary."

"We may have a bit of a problem."

"In what way?" asked Dr Western.

"In the way that the tiles in the centre of the impulse gun are gone," Gary said.

"What do you mean gone?" asked Dr Western, in a slightly stunned, disbelieving way.

"I mean, where they should be, they are not, and in their place, is an area that looks like it has been scorched green." he tried to explain.

"Scorched in what way?" asked Dr Western trying to understand.

"Well," said Gary, doing his best to explain, "you know when you burn something on a tiled surface and it leaves a smoky film? Well, that is what it looks like."

"I mean," he continued, "it is really thick in the centre, and it gets lighter as it radiates out."

"Can you get a sample to bring in and show us?" asked Dr Western.

"I will do better than that," said Gary. "A few of the tiles next to the row of missing ones are loose, and I should be able to pry one away without too much difficulty."

"That would be a great help," said Dr Western.

"I'm here with Gary now, Dr Western," came Tony's voice over the intercom. "I can give him a hand."

"Thanks, Tony. I will see you when you get back inside."

"Dr Western," said Dr Peterson, "I've gone over all the data, and everything seems all right, up until when the impulse gun was fired. Then there was a massive surge of energy."

"Is there any indication as to what may have caused it?" asked Dr Western.

"No," said Dr Peterson, "but it seemed to emanate from the gun itself."

"But how is that possible?" asked Dr Western, more to himself than to anyone who might answer. "I mean, it was calibrated and checked and then rechecked. All the fail safes were in place, and according to the readouts, were working fine."

"Could it have been tampered with in some way?" asked Dr Peterson.

"I don't see how," said Dr Western.

"I mean, the place was as secure as could be, and all the parts that came in were well and truly checked out."

"So, you are saying all the parts were checked, the gun was stable, and all the readouts were within their parameters. Then what happened?" asked Dr Peterson.

"That would seem to be the sixty-four dollar question," said Dr Western. "Maybe we should check the readings once again to see if we missed something."

So, they set about going over all the data again, and when they had finished, Dr Western said, "Well, it all checks out, and I still do not see any obvious signs that might be an indicator as to what happened."

"Maybe this will help answer some questions," said Gary, as he entered the room holding a 300-millimetre square tile, which he promptly handed to Dr Western.

"You're right, Gary. This does look like smoke damage, and this edge here is all pitted whilst the other three side are still smooth," noted Dr Western.

"That's the side that was facing towards the centre, so it was next to the missing tiles, said Gary, hoping to help shed some light on the subject.

"And you say that this green film was on all the tiles?" asked Dr Western.

"Yes," said Gary. "It was really dark in the middle, and it got lighter as it went to the outer edge."

"That is interesting," said Dr Western, as he took the tile over to the electron spectrograph, before placing it inside and switching the machine on.

"Hopefully, we can isolate the trace elements of the green film, and that may help us in determining what actually caused the explosion," he said

After a few moments, the analysis was displayed on the screen.

Dr Western's eyes became a little wider when he saw the results.

"What is it Doc?" asked Gary.

"Well, according to the readout, the green film and the scorched edge actually have traces of Crandinium in them," was his stunned reply.

"But that is one of the most unstable elements known to man," said Dr Peterson. "Why would there be traces of it in the tile?"

"My guess would have to be that the missing tiles were somehow impregnated with Crandinium, and when the impulse gun was fired, the unstable nature of the substance caused it to explode," explained Dr Western.

"But why would you put that stuff in the tiles in the first place?" asked Gary.

"Normally, it is not something you would do, unless you actually wanted an explosion," said Dr Western.

"But why would you want to . . . ahh," said Gary, as he realized who may have been behind it.

"The anti-interference wack-job brigade," he said, not trying to hide the contempt in his voice.

"But wasn't that fellow caught before he could do any damage, the other week?" asked Dr Peterson.

"Maybe we were meant to catch him," said Dr Western.

"What do you mean?" asked Dr Anders.

"Well," said Dr Western, trying to explain, "he could have been a decoy, so that we would think that we had foiled them before they got to the launch site and therefore feel secure in the knowledge that we were safe, when in actuality, the tiles were more than likely already in place."

"But why would they not have been checked when they were first brought in?" asked Dr Peterson.

"Oh, they would have been checked," said Dr Western, "and when it was seen that they were all crates of tiles the same shape and colour, they would have been allowed to enter."

"Also," he continued, "for all we know, there may have been help from within the organization."

"What about all the security checks that are done on everyone?" asked Dr Anders.

"When you bring together an organization as large as the one we did, there are such a vast number of people that, whether it is by accident or design, some things are going to slip through," said Dr Western. "And I am not saying that that is an excuse. I am saying that is the reality."

"So, what do we do now?" asked Dr Anders. "I mean, we can't stay up here forever, and we can't go back until we get comms with Earth. We can't even do the job we were sent up here to do, because the impulse gun is now inoperable."

"Actually," said Dr Western, "the data shows us that the impulse gun will still work if we can replace the tiles, and, as Gary has said, it is still structurally sound, just covered in a film of green smoke."

"So you're saying that we can still use it?" asked Tony.

"Gary," said Dr Western, as he gestured for him to answer.

"I don't see why not," said Gary. "Of course, all the tiles will have to be wiped clean, and we have a crate of spare tiles that can be fitted in place of the missing ones, but once that is done, we're good to go."

"OK, then that's a starting point, said Dr Western.

"I suggest we get started and sort out the other problems that may occur, when we can."

After a while, Dr Western looked up from his data screens, and noticed Dr Anders had a somewhat quizzical look on her face as she sat at her work station.

"Is something wrong?" he asked.

She looked up and replied, "It's just that when I tried to raise the outstation at Ganymede, I was unable to, because it is not there."

"What do you mean? It has been there for almost a year now," replied Dr Western.

"Not the outstation," said Dr Anders, "Ganymede."

"What? Do you mean to say that the shock wave has pushed it away?" asked Gary, trying to comprehend how a Moon that was larger than Mercury could just disappear.

"No," said Dr Anders, "the shock wave would have no effect over that distance. I am saying that Ganymede is not there, yet."

"What do you mean, yet?" asked Tony.

"When I used my co-ordinates to locate it, I could not. Thinking that the blast may have upset the settings, I broadened my search and noted that Ganymede was not the only object that was not where it should be."

"So, using the star charts and calculations on my computer, I was able to find that, although nothing is where it should be at the moment, it is moving there." she explained.

"OK," asked Gary, "if it is 'not there' yet, how long before it is there?"

"At closest estimation," she said, "about 65 million years."

ENCOUNTER

As the skyship approached the exit of the skyhole, Controller Krerbnot turned to Blet and said, "I am glad that your younglings have joined you to watch as we exit the skyhole, Overbeing. For even though it will be different than when we entered, it is nevertheless quite a spectacle."

"Thank you, Controller," replied Blet, "but truth be known, I doubt if any of Zaldark's strongest troops would have been able to stop them once they were told of your offer to join you as we exit."

"A keen mind is a strong mind, Overbeing," said Krerbnot.

"That is true, Controller," replied Blet.

As he now focused on the exit of the skyhole, as it rapidly approached, Krerbnot again noticed that something was not as it should be.

This time, he could see the inside edge of the skyhole seemed to shimmer instead of maintaining a sharp edge.

Then, as they exited, the brilliance of the colours that had been enveloping the ship for the last twelve rotations, fell behind them, to be instantly replaced by the absolute vastness of space.

Whereas, once there had been light of every colour imaginable, now there was the sharpest, deepest, darkest blackness that was illuminated by countless billions of stars, which were like pin holes in the sky.

The change was so severe that it was said that some even went mad, but Krerbnot had not seen any cases himself. He thought it to be a tale to scare younglings and citizens of weak mind.

Although it did not have the colourful beauty of the skyhole, the contrast to what was now being seen was beauty in itself.

"I am always awestruck as to how vast everything seems after leaving the relative confines of the skyhole," said Krerbnot.

"Yes," said Blet, "it is truly amazing."

"Controller Krerbnot," the voice came from one of the technicians.

"Yes, Technician Dseto?" replied Krerbnot.

"We are receiving a transmission from the surveillance ship orbiting our new world," she informed him.

"Very good. Show it on the display screen," said Krerbnot, as he turned to watch it.

"Controller Krerbnot, may the Great Protector watch over you and your core," said the face that was now displayed on the screen.

"And to you as well, Controller Etklalo," replied Krerbnot.

"I trust your journey was a pleasant one," said Etklalo.

"Indeed it was. Thank you," replied Blet.

"Do you have the co-ordinates for me?" he then asked, feeling that the pleasantries had been dealt with.

"Indeed. I am sending them as we speak," said Etklalo.

"I have located three sites that I feel would be best suited—" then, in an almost blinding green flash, the screen went blank.

"Technician Dseto, what has happened?" asked Krerbnot.

"I am not sure, Controller," said Dseto. "All of my systems appear to be functioning correctly," she added.

"Then why can we not receive them?" he asked, growing slightly impatient.

"It would appear, Controller, that they, for some reason, have ceased transmission."

"I think it is time for you to return to our lodgings," said Blet, turning to his three younglings.

As they left, Blet turned to Krerbnot and asked, "What has happened, Controller?"

"I am not sure, Overbeing, but I will find out," he said as he turned back to the technician and asked, "Have you been able to re-establish communication with the surveillance ship, Technician Dseto?"

"Not yet, Controller," replied Dseto, "and just to make sure, I have once again checked my systems, and they are all functioning as they should."

"Then why would the transmission just end?" asked Krerbnot, now becoming frustrated at not having the answer straight away.

"Maybe there is something in the transmission that can explain it, Controller," said Blet.

"You may be right, Overbeing. Dseto, can you replay the message?"

"Of course, Controller," she replied.

After viewing it again, Krerbnot said, "Can you replay the end of the message slowly?"

"Yes, Controller."

As he was watching, Krerbnot suddenly said, "Stop there."

Immediately, the image froze, as the green flash filled the screen.

"Now, go back, slowly," said Krerbnot.

"Yes, Controller," said Dseto once again.

As he was watching, Krerbnot said, "There, what is that?" referring to the image in the viewing portal that was behind Controller Etklalo.

It appeared to be a craft of some kind that looked as though it was shrouded in a green haze.

"Now, go forward, slowly," said Krerbnot.

As they watched, they saw the green haze suddenly and violently expand until it reached Etklalo's ship, and the transmission ended.

"Now, can you run it back again, slowly?"

"Of course, Controller," said Dseto.

Again they all watched as this time the green haze moved away from Etklalo's ship, until it was nothing but a glow around the strange craft, and then, the craft disappeared.

"Stop," said Krerbnot. "Now go forward again."

This time they watched as the strange craft just appeared.

Once again, Krerbnot said, "Stop."

"How can this be?" asked Blet. "Things just cannot be where they were not, a moment before."

"Not only that, Overbeing," said Krerbnot, "but why then did it destroy a defenceless craft, without even trying to contact it?"

"I think these and other questions might best be answered if we had more minds to think on them," said Blet.

"I will summon Commandling Zaldark," he continued, "and I will need yourself and Maintainer Zeral to join me in a meeting with the sayers."

"Very good, Overbeing. When will this meeting take place?" asked Krerbnot.

"I will get adviser Rerkr to ask the sayers when it would be possible to meet with them," replied Blet. "And we will need somewhere for the meeting to take place," he added.

"Of course," said Krerbnot. "I will make sure the meeting room next to the main viewing area is ready."

"Good. I shall summon you in one large time period," said Blet.

"I shall be ready," replied Krerbnot, "and hopefully, we shall be able to find the answers."

"That is what we all hope," said Blet as he turned to head out of the control room, to locate Rerkr.

LONG WAY FROM HOME

"Wait . . . What? No . . . Hang on . . . Stop," said Gary. "You said that the shock wave was not enough to move anything, and now you are saying that things are so far away from where they should be that it is going to take 65 million years for them to get back to where they should be. What do you actually mean?"

"I am not saying that the explosion caused everything to move away," said Dr Anders, "What I am saying, is that since the 'Big Bang', the universe has been expanding, and with the right formula, we can see how fast that expansion is and also we can calculate where things were at any given point in time. According to my calculations, those things are currently where they were 65 million years ago."

No one spoke, as they tried to understand and comprehend what they had just been told.

"So," said Tony, "somehow the universe has shifted backwards 65 million years. Is that what you are trying to tell us?"

"Not the universe . . . us," came Dr Anders' reply.

"What? You're saying we travelled back in time 65 million years?" said Gary. "How could that be even possible?"

"My guess would be that the explosion ripped a hole in the space-time continuum, and we fell through it," replied Dr Anders.

"Well, when you explain it like that, it sounds so obvious. C'mon, Doc, time travel? Surely there has to be another explanation. I mean, it's not possible, is it?" asked a less than sure Gary.

Dr Peterson replied.

"Actually, Gary," he said, "there are those that think that all time coexists, and that it does so by being on different planes. If you had the right circumstance, you could move from one plane to another and, thereby, travel through time. But, as I say, it is only a theory."

"Why . . . ? Uh . . . you . . . I mean . . . how . . . ? It's . . . phew. That's a lot to think about," Gary finally stumbled out.

"So, OK. Let's say we did go back in time. Is there any way to reverse the process?" asked Tony.

"Again, in theory," said Dr Peterson, "if you can find the exact cause, replicate it precisely, then run it in reverse, there is a chance you may be able to get a similar result."

"Fills me with confidence," said a slightly sarcastic Tony.

"So, we are currently in the time of the dinosaurs," said Dr Anders.

"Only trouble is, there may not be any left due to our entry," said Dr Western.

"I thought a meteor wiped them all out," said Gary.

"Yes, well, it may or may not have already hit, and if it has not, it would be the first species wiped out due to human interference," said Dr Western.

"Hmm," said Gary, "well at least now I don't feel so bad about my father having to put down our dog all those years ago."

"So what do we do now?" asked Tony, "Just wait around for the next 65 million years until we get rescued?"

"I think we should make sure that everything is 100 per cent, so that at least we will be fine for our immediate future," said Dr Western, who was not a great supporter of feeling sorry for yourself.

"Gary, how long will it take to replace the tiles?"

"If all the securing points are OK, I would say about three days, and if they are damaged, obviously a little longer," he replied.

"OK, you may as well get started on that, and I will run a few more diagnostic checks on the impulse gun. Drs Peterson and Anders, use this opportunity for information gathering, because, I'm not real sure, but I don't think this situation is going to arise again soon," said Dr Western, again, trying to distract everyone by keeping them busy, as well as trying to sound upbeat and optimistic.

"What's the point?" asked Tony, "I mean, we are stuck here, with the nearest help 65 million years away, and I am pretty sure we did not bring that many rations."

"No we didn't," replied Dr Western in a voice that was stern enough to even surprise himself a little.

"But I thought that we would have brought along a little bit of heart and hope," he continued. "Yes, we are a long way from help, but that does not mean that there is no help at all. I mean, even if the odds are stacked against us, and we only have a small chance of returning, it is still a chance, and I am not giving up. As for food, the replicator is working perfectly well, and worst case scenario, if we do run out of food we can land on the surface and forage."

"You really think we can get back?" asked Dr Anders.

"Dr Peterson . . ." said Dr Western, redirecting the question.

"Theoretically, it is not impossible, but it would take a long time and a lot of luck, to get close to figuring it out," said Dr Peterson.

"Well, it would appear that we may have more than a little time to spare with not too many distractions, and as for luck, the fact that we were not vaporized when the tiles exploded means maybe Hughie is looking out for us." said Gary.

"Besides," he continued, "I always wanted to be a farmer."

"Who is Hughie?" asked Dr Anders.

Then pointing upwards, Gary said, "You know, Hughie, him upstairs, the big boss."

"Please don't take the Lord's name in vain," said Tony, with a not-so-impressed look on his face.

Gary, realizing that the last thing they needed was friction, apologized, then added, "I was just saying, that so far we have been pretty lucky, and as long as we have not used up all of our luck, things just may fall our way."

After a few tense moments, Tony sighed and said, "You're right, I'm sorry. It's just that, phew, this is quite a bit to take in."

"OK then," said Dr Western, "let's get busy, so that at least we will be more prepared in the event of something else happening."

"Yes," said Gary, "you never know when the Martians are going to just drop by."

When he saw that everyone was looking at him slightly bemused, he just raised his hands, palms up, shrugged his shoulders and said, "What? I'm just saying, that's all."

Tony lowered his head as he shook it from side to side and said, "Please, someone get us back."

Gary just continued to smile.

GONE

The pandemonium at Mission Control had started to abate slightly, as people realized they needed to be more methodical as opposed to yelling at each other to try to attain information.

"Steve, do you have anything?" asked Ray Stevens, who was mission co-ordinator and therefore tasked with the job of trying to find out what went wrong.

"Nothing out of the ordinary just yet," replied Steve, who was head of the team monitoring the impulse gun test.

"We've gone over everything we have, and it all seems to be going well up until the explosion."

"Keep checking. There has to be something, and we have to find it."

"Ray," came a voice over his headset. "General Fredrickson wants to speak to you."

"Thanks, Andy. Patch him through."

"Mr Stevens, do we have any idea what the hell just happened yet?" came the voice of someone that sounded like they did not like to be kept waiting for answers.

"Not yet, General, but rest assured, I will find out," said Ray, trying to sound more optimistic than he felt.

"Well rest assured yourself, Mr Stevens," replied the general. "After the amount of time and money that the military has pumped into this project, I would hope that you would find out, and, as I have a meeting with the World Council in five hours, I would also hope that you could do so with some expediency."

"General," said Ray, trying to maintain a calm demeanour, "please do not think for a moment that we are not doing our utmost to try and figure out what went wrong."

"I am not saying that, Mr Stevens. I am merely trying to stress the point that the World Council will want as much intelligence that they can get so that they can make a more informed decision as to what they should do next," replied the general.

"And," he continued, "I am going to need the information first, so that I can then figure out the best way to deliver it."

"OK, General," said Ray, starting to calm down a little. "As soon as we find out anything, we will let you know."

"Thank you, Mr Stevens, and I will call you in four and a half hours for a final briefing before I meet with the World Council," said the general, and he terminated the call before Ray could say anything more.

"Military," said Ray, as he snatched his headset off and felt like throwing it at something hard. "As if we didn't have enough on our plate without having to kowtow to them."

"Yes, well, they did fund a great deal of this project, so I suppose they are just trying to find out where there money has gone," said Steve, doing his best at being diplomatic.

"Or just trying to figure out how best to get troops on the Moon for the ultimate 'air superiority'," said Ray, trying to let off a little more steam without actually smashing something.

"I would think they might be more interested in the weapons capability of the impulse gun rather than anything to do with space travel," said Steve.

"Yeah, if it's not mine, blow it up. Brilliant strategy," said Ray with a wry smile on his face as he looked at Steve.

"OK," said Steve, "now that you've got that out of your system, can we get back to figuring out what happened?"

"You're right," said Ray, as he put his headset back on.

"How you doing, Tony?" he asked of Tony Pearson, the person tasked with checking all video footage they had of the test.

"We may have something," replied Tony.

"What's that?" asked Ray as he approached Tony's work station.

"Right, I will put it up on the main screen so you can see it better," said Tony.

"Now, as you can see, we have a good image looking into the dish of the impulse gun, albeit from the side, because obviously we could not get below the dish, because of the nature of the impulse gun, any satellite in the path of the test would be destroyed."

"So, if we run it forward with audio," he continued, as everyone listened to the last words they heard Dr Western speak, "Firing in five, four, three, two, one."

It was at that moment Tony paused the image.

"At this point, nothing untoward is happening, but now, if we forward one frame at a time," he said, as his hand slowly rotated a dial that could advance images taken at ten frames a second, "you can see here, just as the impulse gun is fired, there is what appears to be, a green haze in the central part of the dish."

"Then, in the next frame, we see a green flash, and in the next frame, all gone, and all that, in two tenths of a second," he said, as he looked at the blank expression on the faces around him.

"Can you run that again please?" said Ray.

Tony played the images again, and three more times afterwards.

"So, how can a blast of that magnitude finish so abruptly with no residual aftershock?" asked Steve.

"Also," said Tony, "where is all the debris?"

"Ray," came Andy's voice over his headset.

"Here, Andy," Ray answered.

"There is someone here you may be interested in speaking to," said Andy.

"Who's that?" asked Ray.

"A man by the name of Drew Betts. He is a professor in astrophysics, and he was invited here to watch the launch," replied Andy.

"That's nice, Andy, but what has this got to do with star gazing?" asked Ray, who realized as soon as he said it, that getting snappy with people trying to help, was not really productive.

"Sorry, Andy. How does he think he can help?" he then said.

"That's OK, Ray," said Andy, knowing that everyone was under a fair amount of stress. "It's just that he says that he may have a theory on the explosion, and he would like to come down and discuss it with you."

"Does he really think he can help?" asked Ray.

"He seems to think that he can," Andy replied.

"OK, send him down. At this stage we need all the help we can get," said Ray.

About a minute later, they were all joined by a middle-aged, bespectacled man, dressed in a suit that looked as though it was so comfortable it had not been taken off for a week.

When he spoke, it was not with a loud voice, but one with a quiet confidence in that what he said was sure to be correct.

"Mr Stevens?" he asked, whilst trying to look at everyone at the same time to see who might respond.

"That would be me," said Ray.

"Allow me to introduce myself," said the professor, extending his arm. "I am Professor Drew Betts, and I am head lecturer at Central University."

"Obviously, we need any help we can get, Professor, and please do not think that I am trying to be flippant, but how do you see this event to be related to your studies, when the only connection I can see, is that it took place in space?" asked Ray.

"Well," replied the professor, "one of the areas in my field of studies is explosions in space, their effect, and what caused them."

"What, you mean like when rockets explode after a faulty launch?" asked Tony, not really sure what to think.

"No, I mean deep space explosions, whether they be from impact, energy build up due to chemical reaction, or an implosion caused by a collapsing star," he explained.

"So which category do you think this would come under?" asked Ray.

"From the images I have seen, I would probably have to say two categories," said the professor.

"I see," said Ray, "what brings you to that conclusion?"

"Well," said the professor, feeling as though he was about to address a senior class in their final semester lectures, "as we can see, there did not appear to be an impact, and if we look closely at the images, just as the device is activated the tiles at the base appear to blister slightly. Then, we see the green haze that turns into a bright flash before everything suddenly disappears."

"Yes, we can see that, Professor, but what does it mean?" asked Ray.

"If I had to guess, because that is all I can do at this stage, I would say, that the blistering and green flash are the fuel source igniting and that the explosion was so abrupt and powerful it collapsed in on itself," explained the professor.

"OK, just a couple of things," said Ray. "The surface of the dish was made of mirror-polished ceramic Titrilium tiles that are totally inert, and in every explosion I have seen the energy has always spread out, not in."

"Yes, Mr Stevens, Titrilium is inert, which leads me to think that the tiles we see blistering were not as they should have been," said the professor.

"What do you mean? Not as they should be?" asked Tony.

"For there to be an explosion like the one we see here you would need to use a material with a very unstable composition, and the only one I can think of that would give us this result is Crandinium," replied the professor.

"That could not be possible, Professor, because everything that was brought onsite had to pass through at least three check points," said Ray.

"I do not doubt that, Mr Stevens, but when it was checked, was it checked for content or composition?" asked the professor.

"What do you mean?" asked Ray.

"I mean, in the right hands, Crandinium, although unstable, can be made to look like many other elements, and without an electron spectrogram it would be very difficult to tell the difference," he explained.

"So, how can we tell now?" asked Tony.

"Well, as we can't check the debris from the explosion," said the professor, "can we check to see if there are any tiles that may have not been used?"

"Andy," said Ray into his microphone, "can you get security to go to Warehouse Three and check to see if there are any spare tiles for the impulse gun."

"On it," said Andy.

"Now, Professor," said Ray, "what you said about the explosion collapsing in on itself—could you elaborate please?"

"Certainly," he said. "It would be the same principle as when a star has used up all its energy and then collapses, creating a black hole. The energy from the explosion would first expand but would be drawn back by an immense gravitational pull."

"A black hole," was all Tony could say.

"Or conditions very similar," said Professor Betts.

"But I thought the nature of a black hole was such that it engulfed all its surrounds," said Ray.

The professor then went on to explain.

"If it was an object the size of a star, I would say yes, and if it were the size of a star, I can guarantee you we would not be able to discuss this right now."

"Furthermore," he continued, "I would say that if it happened on Earth, it would have had enough energy to obliterate a small city."

"How small?" asked Tony.

"One approximately 20 kilometres across," replied the professor, "and in its place, would be a 10 kilometre deep hole."

Everyone was silent, as they tried to imagine such a scenario.

"So," said Tony, more in hope than anything else, "there would be no hope that anyone could have been maybe thrown clear and survived?"

"There would be no hope at all, because as I have said, although the initial force of the blast was outwards, it was soon compressed into an area of microscopic proportions."

"If it is any consolation," he continued, "they would not have known what happened."

"Ray," came a voice over his headset.

"Here, Andy," Ray replied.

"I just heard from security, and they have found a pack of five spare tiles."

"OK, can you get them taken over to Lab Number Two and have Richard run a scan on them?"

"Do we know what we are looking for?" asked Andy.

"Crandinium or traces thereof," said Ray.

"Wow, I will let them know and get back to you as soon as I hear something," said Andy.

"Thanks, Andy," said Ray.

"So what do we do now?" asked Steve.

"I think we should go over everything again to make sure we have not missed anything," said Ray, "and then when we hear from Richard, I will have more of an idea of what to tell General Fredrickson."

"Professor Betts, would you mind sticking around for a while until we know for sure that we are on the right track."

"Of course," said the professor.

"OK guys," said Ray, "we have got work to do, and hopefully, we will find enough answers to keep General Fredrickson and the World Council happy."

"I'm not sure that guy has ever been happy," said Steve.

"Yeah, I know, but all we can do is try," said Ray as he was wondering where this investigation might lead him.

COURSE TAKEN

"So what do we know about this strange craft?" asked Elder Glerci, as the assembled group sat around the table in the meeting room that Krerbnot had made ready.

"There was not much we could see in the images we have that would tell us anything about it—only that it seemed to appear out of nothing and that it slightly resembles the old war stations of Satembi 5," said Controller Krerbnot.

"You have seen these war stations, Controller?"

This time the question was asked by Elder Bnotkl.

"Not myself, but when I showed the images to Commandling Zaldark, it was he that said it was so," replied Krerbnot.

"Is this so, Commandling Zaldark?" was Bnotkl's next question.

"I did make that statement, Elder Bnotkl, but as we all know, the war fleet of Satembi 5 was crushed and then totally disbanded, so it could not be from there," he explained.

"However," he continued, "it does have a similarity in appearance."

"So, are you saying that this is a craft of war?" asked Elder Glerci.

"Without a closer inspection, it is hard to say," said Zaldark, "but I do not know of many peaceful crafts that would attack and destroy an unarmed vessel without warning or provocation."

"Controller, you say this craft appeared as though out of nothing. Could you explain what you mean?" asked Elder Zotstot.

"It is as I say," said Krerbnot. "On the images we have one moment it is not there and the next moment, it is."

"Could it be that it arrived in the area at such a great speed that you could not see and that somehow it was able to stop so suddenly that it gave the appearance of just materializing as though out of nothing?" asked Zotstot.

This time, it was Maintainer Zeral who replied.

"If I may answer that, Elder. I have worked on all manner of craft in my time, and one thing has always been certain and that is, when you are working with objects that move at such vast speeds, you cannot get them to come to a complete stop without some residual motion. The images I saw led me to believe that the craft was absolutely motionless."

"Could something have been blocking the image so that we could not see it?" Zotstot then asked.

"Again, referring to the images we have seen," said Krerbnot, "nothing would suggest that the craft was being obscured."

"The reason I ask," said Zotstot, "is that many cycles prior there were patrols through the vast emptiness of the plains of my homeland, and when those patrols returned they would say, many times over, that although there was nothing to be seen attacks from marauders would happen as though they had appeared out of nowhere. They were able to conceal themselves so well that even the most observant scout would have difficulty in noticing where they were."

"Now, I do not mean that this attack was performed by marauders," continued Zotstot, "what I am saying, is that just because we do not see something does not mean that it is not there."

"I am sorry, Elder," said Maintainer Zeral, "but I do not see how it is possible to hide behind something that is not there and not be seen."

"I say this, Maintainer Zeral, because our knowledge seekers are developing a device that when activated is capable of hiding something by making light actually bend around it so that, although you may be looking directly at an object, you see images from beside and behind it, making it possible to conceal yourself behind something that is not there."

"I have heard some speak of this," said Controller Krerbnot, "they call it a 'light blanketing device'."

"That is correct, Controller," said Zotstot.

"They have not yet perfected it," he continued, "but we have been assured that it is possible, and, if what you are saying is so, then perhaps others have found a way to completely conceal large objects in plain sight."

"Then how can we defeat an enemy that we cannot see?" asked Zeral.

"With great caution," said Zotstot.

"So, we must proceed slowly and be ready to act quickly," said Krerbnot.

"That is correct, Controller," said Zaldark," and also act in a way that will put us in a superior position."

"And how do you see that we can do that?" asked Zeral.

"Information that we have about our new world is that it has a small, desolate world which could only be used for mineral excavation orbiting it," said Krerbnot.

"If we could approach in such a way as to keep this world between us and the craft," he continued, "we should be able to get close enough to gain more information."

Elder Glerci then asked, "Is it possible for this to be done without being detected?"

Maintainer Zeral answered.

"I do not know of any device that can see through worlds, so I would think that if we do as Controller Krerbnot says and use our long range detectors so that we can position ourselves correctly, we should be able to arrive undetected."

Commandling Zaldark then said, "If we can do this, it will be a great advantage to us, for the more information you have on your enemy, the better the chance you have of finding a way to defeat them."

"Controller Krerbnot, do we possess the necessary weapons to be able to defend ourselves should the need arrive?" asked Elder Glerci.

"I ask this," he continued, "because there are a great number of citizens on board, and I do not wish to place them in unnecessary danger."

"Elder Glerci," replied Krerbnot, "this trip is full of unforeseen dangers. Some we have tried to prepare for, others we could not. But I can assure you that we have a weapons array we will be able to use to defend ourselves against quite a formidable foe."

"Hopefully, it will not come to that," said Elder Glerci.

"That is what we all hope," said Zaldark, "but it is better to be ready and act first than to wait for your opponent to strike the first blow and then have to retaliate from a weaker position."

"Then may the Great Protector guide us and deliver us the best outcome," said Elder Glerci.

BE PREPARED

"How you doing out there, Gary?" asked Dr Western.

"Yeah, not too bad," Gary replied. "It's a little more cumbersome than I expected, but it is coming along OK."

"So, are you still going to be able to get them all in?" was Dr Western's next question.

"There's no worry there, Doc," replied Gary, "It's just that it is probably going to take me a couple of days extra."

"That's all right, it's not like we have a schedule to keep," came Dr Western's response.

"I might finish the last three on this row and come back in," said Gary, "because my union says that I have to have at least three cups of coffee a day, and we don't want to upset the union."

"No, we would not want that," said Dr Western, realizing as soon as he had said it that he was starting to pick up traits of Gary's sense of humour.

"Dr Anders," said Dr Western as he saw her entering the control room, "How are your observations going?"

"It is truly remarkable, and please, can you call me Julie?" she replied.

"Of course, Julie, and please, call me Raul," he answered.

"Have you made any new, or should I say old, discoveries?" Raul then asked.

"Well, once I was able to curb my enthusiasm to try to look at everything at the same time," she said, "I was able to find numerous stars and even some galaxies in their infancy, and I think I may have found a couple of stars that are no longer there—well, in our time anyway."

"Also," she continued, "I have picked up on something that I think I will need to do some more study on."

"Nothing too severe I hope," said Raul.

"I don't think so," she said, "just an anomaly I want to check on."

"So, you will be one step ahead of your contemporaries when we get back," Raul then said.

Julie looked at him and asked, "Do you really think we can get back?"

"Well," he replied, "so far in my life I have never been on a trip that I could not return from, and I don't want to give up hope and say this is the first because I also think that without hope you do not have a great deal."

"Yes, as my father used to say, being optimistic is half the battle," Julie said.

"It's a good way to be," replied Raul.

"I just wish he was still here to see that I finally got into space," Julie then said.

"I'm sorry to hear that," said Raul. "If you don't mind my asking, how long ago did he pass?"

"It was seven years ago," she said. "He started complaining about headaches, and when we were finally able to convince him that he should go and see a doctor, he was diagnosed with brain cancer. Four months later, we had his funeral."

Raul, unsure of what to say, said nothing and just let Julie keep talking.

"He was actually the one that got me interested in studying space," she continued, "as he was always trying to share in his enthusiasm of the fascination of space and its vastness and complexity, and then when he bought me my first telescope when I was thirteen, I knew that's all I ever wanted to do."

"My father was always working on old cars," said Raul. "My mother would get so cross with him if he put even the slightest mark of grease in the house, but he would just smile, wink at me, and then say to my mother, 'It's all right, dear. Even Leonardo Da Vinci sometimes made a mess'. Of course, my mother would not see the funny side, and would say things like, 'Then maybe you should get Leonardo Da Vinci to clean up after you'."

"But one thing I do remember, though," he continued, "is that he always made sure everything was done correctly and that he always used to say, 'check it twice, do it once', and I think that is where I learned to become a little bit of a perfectionist."

"How do you become a little bit of a perfectionist?" asked Julie, with a wry smile on her face.

Raul gave a slight chuckle, then answered.

"The first time you try to correct your mother for doing something that you think should be done better, quickly teaches you that sometimes your perception of perfection may not be the best course of action to take."

Julie laughed and then said, "Yes, I grew up knowing that my mother was in charge, and although I never heard them argue, I knew Mom was continually frustrated with my father for the way he cluttered the house with telescopes and star charts and about a zillion books on space and all things associated with it."

"That's quite a lot of books," Raul said with a smile.

"Yes," replied Julie, "we were never short of reading material."

"And, if I may ask, where is your mother now?" inquired Raul.

Julie replied, "She is actually in a retirement village in the lakes district of England, a place called Windermere."

"That sound rather picturesque," remarked Raul.

"Yes," said Julie, "and she really does like it there."

"Also," Julie continued, "she can't understand why she did not move there years earlier."

"That seems to be the way, though," said Raul, "we often realize far too late what it is that we really want."

"Well, right about now," said Julie," I want a cup of tea. So if you will excuse me, I think I will go and have one."

"Of course," said Raul with a grin on his face, "and I better get back to my readouts."

"Would you like a cup of tea or coffee?" asked Julie.

"No, I'm fine thanks," Raul replied, "I am not a huge coffee drinker, and I already had one a little earlier."

"OK," said Julie, "I will be in the galley if I am needed."

And with that, she turned to head off and make herself a cup of tea.

"Hey, Doc."

Raul turned to see Gary enter through the door on the other side of the room.

"Gary," he said, "So everything is going OK out there?"

"Yeah," Gary answered, "it's like I said, it's not too bad, although it is very tiring and hard, so I might have to put in for a pay rise."

"OK, I will bring it up at the next board meeting," said Raul, realizing that he was sinking further and further into the depths of Gary's sense of humour.

"That's great, Doc," said Gary, "and to show my appreciation, I will even make you a cup of coffee."

"No, that's fine, Gary. I had one not that long ago," Raul replied.

"Righty-oh. I'll be back in a little while," said Gary as he headed towards the galley.

As he entered the galley, Gary saw that Julie was making herself a drink.

"Dr Anders," he said, "how are you doing with your observations?"

"Fine," she replied, "and, as I have just said to Raul, please call me Julie."

"Hmm," said Gary," he must think pretty highly of you."

"Why do you say that?" asked Julie.

"Well, it's just that he is a pretty closed person, so to be on a first-name basis is something that should not be taken very lightly," Gary explained.

"I mean," he continued," there are a few people I know of who have worked with him for years and still refer to him as Dr Western."

"Well, I find him very approachable," said Julie.

"Oh, don't get me wrong," said Gary, "once you get to know him, he is one of the nicest people you will ever get to meet. It is just that until that time he is usually fairly guarded."

"Why is that?" asked Julie. "Did something happen?"

"I don't think that it is really for me to say," said Gary. "If he wants to discuss his life with you, that should be his choice, not mine."

"Oh please, don't think that I was trying to pry," said Julie in an apologetic tone.

"No, you're right," replied Gary. "It's just that I have known him for a number of years, and I count myself lucky enough to be one of the people who have the privilege of calling him a friend, although at times I do get a little overprotective."

"How did you get to know him?" asked Julie.

"It was about thirteen years ago," said Gary. "I was a police patrolman, and I had been tasked with delivering some news to him, and there was something about the guy that made you think that he was just a decent person."

"Anyway, we got to talking, and I knew my police career was not what I really wanted after all, and, long story short, a few months later, I was working in the Doc's department on the space program."

"Haven't really looked back since," he concluded.

"So, what's the Julie Anders story?" he then asked.

"Oh, you know, the usual, small-town girl, lure of the city lights, fame and fortune, hoping to catch myself a millionaire and be a kept woman," she said as she looked at Gary with an ever-broadening grin on her face.

"And I thought I was the funny one," said Gary with a feigned frown.

"Depends on your perception of funny," was Julie's retort.

"Ouch," said Gary, "I think I just got burned."

"Sorry," Julie said with the remnants of a smile still on her face, "It's just that I think I inherited my father's sense of humour."

"That's OK," said Gary, "Don't ever apologise for trying to make people smile."

"Gosh, it looks like everyone has had the same idea."

Gary and Julie both turned towards the voice, to see Tony and Dr Peterson enter the room.

"Good morning, afternoon, or evening," said Gary, "or whatever time zone you have your clocks set to."

"I think that if we use the time zone that we had when we took off," said Dr Peterson, thinking he was being helpful by being the realist that he was, "it is actually mid-morning."

"That's all right, Dr Peterson, I was just having a joke," explained Gary, realizing that Dr Peterson was a person who took things far too seriously and literally.

"Oh, yes, I see," said Dr Peterson. "That would be humorous."

"I actually know a joke," he then added. "Would you like to hear it? It is quite funny."

"Sure," said Gary. "I am always up for a laugh."

"Very well," said Dr Peterson, "here it is."

"Why would you never tell a ghost a secret?" he asked.

"I don't know. Why?" asked Gary sceptically.

"Because they are transparent, and therefore everyone would have the ability to see right through them," Dr Peterson replied.

Julie thought that the joke was so bad she could not help but burst into laughter.

"Yes," Dr Peterson responded, "it is quite a funny joke, isn't it?"

"Well, let's just say it was not quite what I was expecting," said Julie when she was able to compose herself.

"I remember when I was first told this joke," said Dr Peterson, feeling the need as a mathematician to actually explain the joke, "I did not think that it was all that funny, but after a while, I thought that yes, you can see through what we perceive to be spirits, and that's when I started to view it as a funny joke."

Gary just said, "Yeah, you might just need to work on your presentation."

"What do you mean?" asked Dr Peterson.

"It's not only how you tell a joke," explained Gary, "but you should not really explain it in detail afterwards."

"But what if they do not understand it?" asked Dr Peterson.

"Sometimes," said Gary, "that is the funniest part."

"I don't think I know what you mean," said Dr Peterson.

"And I don't think that I understand why we are talking about the intricacies of comic relief when we should be concentrating on what we need to do to get out of here," said Tony, in a tone that left no one in doubt as to his feelings on the matter.

"It's OK," said Gary, trying to ease the tension that suddenly descended, "We're only having a bit of fun."

"Yes, and I am sure that in your mind, fun is what makes the world go round," replied Tony as he took his coffee and proceeded to head out of the room.

Dr Peterson then said, "Maybe he is right. Perhaps we should be concentrating more on trying to figure out how to get back."

"I don't really think that taking a short break every now and then is going to matter all that much," said Gary.

"If anything," he continued, "it will help to revitalize you. So don't you worry about it, Dr Peterson. You just enjoy your coffee, and I will have a talk to Tony later."

"Very well," replied Dr Peterson, "if you say so, but he did seem a little perturbed."

"Yes, I think that might just be Tony being Tony," said Gary.

"But, like I said, I will have a talk to him later and try to calm him down."

"If you think that is best," said Dr Peterson.

"Yes, I think so," said Gary.

"Now, how are you going with your calculations, Dr Peterson? Are we any closer to getting back?" Gary then asked light-heartedly.

"I would not go so far as to say that we are much closer to getting back," Peterson replied, "but, because of our isolation and the lack of outside distractions, I am coming up with some interesting formulas and that maybe I might be able to find something that could help us."

"Well, keep at it, Dr Peterson, because I think that if anyone can find a way back, it is you," said Gary, trying to build up his self-confidence.

"Thank you, Gary, that is very kind of you to say so," said Dr Peterson, feeling a little more self-assured.

"That's quite all right," said Gary. "Now, if you will excuse me, I might go and have a chat with Tony and try to calm him down a bit."

"Good luck," said Julie.

"Thanks," replied Gary as he headed back into the control room, "I might need it."

"Need what?" asked Raul, as he heard, then saw, Gary enter the room.

"I was just saying I might need a little luck trying to calm Tony down," Gary explained.

"Yes, he did seem a little tense when he walked through," said Raul.

"But then," he continued, "it is the same for us all. It's just that we all handle it a bit differently."

"True dat," said Gary.

"Excuse me?" said Raul with an extremely quizzical look on his face.

"Sorry, Doc," said Gary. "It's a street term from my days on the force. It's just another way of saying that what you have said is correct."

"Oh, I see," said Raul.

"Sorry, Doc. I will try to remember to speak English from now on," said Gary with a grin.

"That might help," replied Raul.

"Anyway," Gary then asked, "did Tony say where he was going?"

"He said he was going to check on the core," answered Raul.

"OK, I might duck down and have a quick chat with him," said Gary as he headed towards the stairs that would take him down to the propulsion room.

When he arrived, he saw Tony typing on the keypad that controlled the thruster motors.

"What's this? Thinking of taking it for a spin?" asked Gary.

"Everything is a joke to you, isn't it?" Tony snapped back. "You make out like this is just some big adventure, and that when we wake up tomorrow, we will all be able to jump in our cars and head home."

"Well, I got some news for you, Dorothy," Tony continued. "Kansas is 65 million years away and clicking your heels together ain't gonna get us there."

"Yes, well, I would not have thought that jumping down each other's throats was being particularly helpful either," replied Gary. "OK, sure. I like to goof around, "but I am just trying to make it easier for everyone by being in a relaxed mood rather than go insane with worry about our situation. It's just that we are all in this together. So the more we work together maybe we will find a way back. I mean, the odds are about a gajillion to one against, but still, any chance is better than no chance."

Tony finally said, with a sigh of resignation, "You're right. It's just that I feel so helpless, you know. When I was first approached about this project, I thought, now here's a challenge, but I also knew that if you asked me to land this craft on a row boat in zero visibility I would say OK. Also, if you asked me to fly this through the eye of a needle, I would say too easy. But, ask me to take us back home, and I can't do it."

"No one is asking you to take us back home," said Gary. "What I am asking you is that you help us to work as a team, and who knows, maybe you will get the chance to take us back home."

Then Gary just waited for a response from Tony.

Eventually, Tony said, "Yeah, you're right. I will just finish what I'm doing here and then go back up and start trying to be a little more helpful with everyone."

"That would be good," said Gary.

"But I would like you to do one thing for me," said Tony.

"What's that?" asked Gary.

"Don't let Dr Peterson tell any more jokes," Tony said with a pleading look on his face.

Gary laughed, maybe more out of tension relief rather than what was actually said, then replied, "Yes, I think that would be a lot easier on everyone."

WHAT NEXT?

"Ray, this is Inspector Peter Watts and Deputy Assistant Stuart Neville from IMPol [investigative branch of military intelligence]," said the project coordinator, Sheilla Henry, as she introduced everyone.

The two men she had introduced were tall and from the cut of their suits both physically active. Their short haircuts told you that they were more than likely in some form of service—in this case the military police.

The inspector, even though he was closing in on forty, gave the impression of a man that could take on and more than likely beat many people half his age. His assistant at fifteen years his junior still had youth on his side.

"They would just like to ask you a few questions regarding what happened."

"Of course," said Ray, "I'll help in any way I can."

"Right. I will leave you to it, and please, do not hesitate to ask, if there is anything that you need," said Sheilla as she turned to head back to her office and what seemed like an ever insurmountable load of work that needed to be done since what was being referred to as the "incident" occurred.

"Now, Mr Stevens," said Inspector Watts, after he had watched Sheilla depart, "what can you tell us about what happened?"

"Well, probably not much more than I told Sheilla and General Fredrickson," said Ray as he gestured toward a nearby table so that they might sit and be a little more comfortable.

"Yes, I have read your report," said the inspector, "but what I need to know is everything that happened leading up to the incident and your insight to the internal workings of this project to try to determine how it could have been possible to arrive at this outcome."

"Like I said, I will help in any way I can," replied Ray.

"OK," said Inspector Watts, as he referred to his notebook that he had placed on the table.

"Now, you say that the explosion could have been caused by tiles made of Crandinium. Are you sure that it was not caused by some other means?"

"Well," said Ray, "we went over all the data and everything was performing as it should have been prior to the explosion.

"Also," he continued, "we examined all the video images that we had, and we could see no impact of any kind."

Deputy Neville then asked, "So by impact do you mean like a missile or another space vessel?"

"No, what I mean," explained Ray, "is that over the last 100 years we have cluttered space with so many non-returnable items, ranging from satellites as big as a car to things like nuts and bolts, that it is actually becoming more hazardous to orbit Earth than it is to fly to another planet."

"Of course," he continued, "it has been getting better since they started the space debris clean-up program twenty years ago and we are able to track over 95 per cent of all man-made clutter, but there are also meteorites that are travelling all over the universe."

"Oh, I see," said Deputy Neville. "Please, go on."

"Well, we could see no impact, and it appeared that the blast seemed to emanate from the centre of the impulse gun," said Ray.

"Then, when we found the spare tiles that were to have been used in the dish of the impulse gun and learned that they were made of Crandinium, we knew that someone must have been able to place some tiles on the craft and that those tiles had reacted when the impulse gun had been fired."

"So, how is it that these tiles would have been able to be used without someone noticing?" asked Inspector Watts.

"Well, without running them through an electron spectrograph it could be fairly difficult, as Crandinium can be made to look like so many other things," explained Ray.

"And where did the tiles come from?" Watts asked.

"As far as I know they only come from one manufacturer, and Sheilla would be able to give you that information," said Ray.

"Would someone have been able to bring them on site without anyone knowing?" asked Deputy Neville.

"Every delivery, no matter what size, is checked three times before it is allowed on site, and a crate the size of the one holding the tiles would not have been able to be snuck in tucked away in a lunch box," replied Ray.

"And was anyone allowed to bring extra equipment on site?" Deputy Neville then asked.

"Every piece of personal equipment brought on site had to pass through the same security checks," said Ray.

"And were those checks the same for everyone?" asked Inspector Watts.

"Everyone," replied Ray, "although, there would be the odd occasion when the crew would bring in specialized equipment that would be sealed in containers that could not be continuously opened and closed back up again due to the delicate and sensitive nature of its components, but whoever brought these items in could guarantee that they could vouch for the items that were packed inside."

"Did you ever receive threats or warnings about what might happen?" asked Deputy Neville.

"Not so much directly," Ray said. "Mainly there were insinuations from the crackpots at the Anti-Interference League."

"Yes, we will be having a chat with Mr Rogerson later on," said the inspector.

"Also," he continued, "I would like the details on Mr Strand, so we can pay him a visit and try to find out how he was able to gain access so easily to the facility and whether he was working alone or not."

"Of course," said Ray, "security will have all that."

"Unfortunately," he added, "they had to release him, as he apparently has democratic rights, and the use of torture is illegal."

"Indeed, is there anything else you can think of that could help?" said the inspector, not wishing to comment on Ray's last statement.

"I don't think so," said Ray, trying to go over everything he could recall about the incident in about two seconds.

"Very well," said Inspector Watts getting to his feet, "if you think of anything, no matter how trivial it may seem, please do not hesitate to call," and he handed Ray his card.

"Shall do," said Ray, as he then watched the two men turn and head back in the direction of Sheilla's office.

"Where to now?" asked Deputy Neville.

"I think we will just get a few details from Sheilla and then go visit Mr Strand," the inspector replied.

* * *

"Mr Strand," said Inspector Watts, holding out his ID so that the person opening the door was able to see it.

"I am Inspector Watts and this is Deputy Neville. We are from IMPol, and I was wondering if we could have a talk."

"OK, what's IMPol?" asked the unextraordinary figure of Graham Strand.

On first impressions, to say that he was average would have been an understatement.

He was not a large man by any stretch of the imagination and the way he stood, as if it was not fair that gravity was making him use energy to remain upright, did not really create an outstanding first impression.

He even had a way of making his clothes look so plain that they gave the impression that everything had been bought in bulk and that, if you were to check his wardrobe, it would surely be filled with identical items.

Even the short question he asked gave Inspector Watts the feeling that to speak to people was an effort for him.

"We are from the Investigative branch of the Military Police," he replied.

"I am not actually in the army, so what makes you think I have to answer to you?" asked Mr Strand with a sneering smile on his face.

"Well," replied Inspector Watts, "as it was a military facility that you broke into, it gives us jurisdiction, and the fact that we are working very closely with the FBI means that if you do not want to co-operate with us, they would love to place you in a federal facility until they get around to questioning you. So, I was wondering if we might just come in and have a chat."

Staring people down was not one of Graham Strand's strong points, so after a few seconds he just grunted in reply, "You better come in then," before he opened the door all the way and stood back to allow them entry.

"Thank you," said Inspector Watts as he and Deputy Neville entered.

"I've already told the police everything," said Strand, as he then led them into the living room.

"Yes, but we would just like to see if maybe you have remembered something else," said the inspector.

"Something like what?" asked Strand.

"Like, who was it you were working with," said the inspector.

"I already told them. I was working alone," said Strand. "I just wanted to prove to the league that I could do something like that, so that I could be counted on, if they ever needed someone of action," Strand added.

Looking at Strand slumped in his couch, action man was not the term that Inspector Watts would have used, as Strand looked more like a puppet waiting for his strings to be pulled.

"How did you gain entry?" asked the inspector, "and please do not say 'as I already told them', as we were not there and we do not know what you told anyone," which was not entirely true, as both the inspector and Deputy Neville had read the record of interview that had taken place between Strand and the police, but he thought it might be a useful ploy to try and throw Strand off balance a little.

"As I alr . . . Sorry," said Strand, as he was starting to get a little more nervous as he usually did when speaking to authority figures, "I was able to get in through a gate on the perimeter fence that was unlocked."

"That was lucky," said Deputy Neville, "I mean, you just happening to be there as the gate was unlocked and no guard patrolling."

"I guess it was lucky," replied Strand.

"I'm just a little curious about one thing though," said the inspector.

"What's that?" asked Strand.

"If it was just luck that the gate was unlocked, how had you planned to get in?" the inspector asked.

"What?" said Strand, with a surprised look on his face, as he did not really expect the question.

"If you did not know that the gate was going to be unlocked, how were you expecting to gain entry into the compound?" asked the inspector again. "Were you going to climb the three—metre razor wire-topped fence with no gloves? Were you going to tunnel your way in without the use of a shovel? Were you going to hijack a truck and force your way in, even though you have never had a driver's license? Did you expect to walk through the front gate without anyone giving you a second glance, or did you go to that gate because someone told you it was going to be unlocked?" he finished leaning slightly forward and staring directly at Strand.

"I told you, I was just walking past and saw the gate was unlocked and went in," said Strand, starting to move around a little uneasily in his seat.

"Who called you just before you went to the base," asked Deputy Neville, making sure that Strand could not just focus on one person at all times.

A look of guilt came over Strand's face as he tried to evade giving an answer.

"How do you know I had a phone call?" he asked, feeling more and more unsure of himself the further the conversation went on.

"Like I said," explained Inspector Watts, using language that Strand would be familiar with, "we are working very closely with the FBI, and they are more than willing to share information. So I will ask you again, who called you just before you went to the base?"

"That was no one—I mean, it was just a friend," said Strand trying to bluff his way through the question.

"I get the feeling," said Inspector Watts, "that you won't be too surprised if I said I don't believe you. So tell me, who made the phone call and, if you don't cooperate, I place a call to a colleague in the Bureau, and you spend a long time getting free room and board with lots of other men in a very secure environment."

Although it was a bluff, the inspector was fairly certain that the weak nature of Strand would come to the fore.

He was correct.

After a few seconds of looking at first Inspector Watts, then Deputy Neville and back again, Strand thought he saw his options running out.

"What sort of deal can you give me if I tell you?" Strand asked.

Inspector Watts looked at him and thought that he must have been watching too many police shows.

"I'm not in a position to offer any deals, but if you cooperate, I will make sure that I tell the relevant people," said the inspector, hoping to make it seem to Strand that he was trying to help him.

After a few more seconds, Strand sat forward in his seat and finally said, "It was a couple of months ago. I got a phone call from someone that said that they were a friend, and they had noticed me at a couple of league meetings and thought that I could be of great assistance to them in taking the league to the next level."

"What did they mean by next level?" asked Deputy Neville.

"I think it was to be more active, rather than just talking," said Strand.

"So, it was Rogerson who organized it?" asked Inspector Watts.

"No," replied Strand with a hint of contempt in his voice.

"Rogerson is weak, and the sooner he is replaced, the better," he added.

"OK, then who was it that called you?" asked the inspector.

"He did not say, because he did not want to incriminate me if they were caught," replied Strand.

After this last statement, Inspector Watts realized just how much intelligence Strand actually lacked.

"Right," said the inspector, "so what was it that they wanted you to do?"

"They told me to see if I could get to the office and get the plans for the launch rockets, and that way, we would be able to say that we were able to sabotage them and the launch would have to be cancelled," said Strand.

"And how did you know where the office was?" asked Deputy Neville.

"I was told that once I got through the gate, it was the long, two-story building, 150 metres away on my left, and that the plans would be in an office on the second floor," Strand said.

"And how did you know which office to go to?" asked the inspector.

"I was told it would be the one marked 'private, do not enter,'" replied Strand.

"Fine," said Inspector Watts as he gestured to Deputy Neville that they should leave.

"I think we have taken up enough of your time Mr Strand, although the police will need to contact you again and retake your statement. I believe we have enough information for now."

"So what will happen to me now?" asked Strand, getting to his feet.

"For the time being, nothing—but I warn you, do not try to leave town and do not try to contact anyone from the league. If you remember anything else, it would be in your best interest to let us know as soon as possible," said the inspector, trying to make sure that Strand remained unsure and scared.

"Yes, of course," said Strand.

As they were walking back to the car, Deputy Neville asked the inspector, "What do you think?"

"I think the guy is obviously so gullible he did not realize he was being used as a decoy," said the inspector. "What we have to ask ourselves now, though, is who it was that called him."

"Could it have been more than one person?" asked Deputy Neville.

"There is that possibility," said the inspector, "but the more people who were actually there could increase their chances of being found out, so I would say that we would only be looking for one person on site."

"Well, that narrows it down to about three hundred," said Deputy Neville.

"So we better keep busy then," said the inspector.

"I think we should go and have a talk with Mrs Western," he then said.

"What? Surely you don't think Dr Western would sabotage his own project," said Deputy Neville.

"Not really," replied the inspector, "but he may have been contacted or threatened by someone and not have taken it seriously and not think to let anyone know."

"You really think so?" asked the deputy.

"Well, we'll know after we talk to Mrs Western, won't we?" said the inspector as he opened the car door and got inside.

ENEMY FORTRESS

As their ship started to slow, so that they could remain hidden from the view of the Moonshaker by staying on the far side of the Moon, Controller Krerbnot first noticed the dull colorization of the Earth due to the dust cloud enveloping it.

"What is that?" he asked out loud but not to anyone in particular.

"Technician Dseto," he then said, "can you check to see why it is this way?"

"Of course, Controller," came the reply.

"Are we sure we know where the other craft is?" asked Krerbnot.

This time, it was Technician Zetkr who spoke.

"Our scanners had them on the far side of the world as we were approaching, and it appears that they are rotating continually, Controller."

"How long before they are back on this side of the world?" Krerbnot then asked.

"One half of one long time section," Zetkr replied.

"Will we be able to scan them without being detected as they next go past?" was Krerbnot's next question.

"I think that because we will be so close to this small mineral world and they will be so far away, it would be extremely difficult for them to detect us," said Zetkr.

"Controller Krerbnot, I have analyzed the shroud around our new world," said Technician Zetkr.

"And what did you find?" asked Krerbnot.

"It appears to be of mineral composition that has reached out to be approximately 100 Mitnars [1,200 metres] thick," answered Zetkr.

Overbeing Blet, who was standing toward the back of the control room next to Commandling Zaldark, then asked, "But why were we not told of this dust cloud before we left Yendor?"

"Because it has not been there before," replied Krerbnot.

"So how would it just suddenly appear?" Blet then asked.

"I would think that the same force that destroyed our surveillance ship has caused the dust cloud," said Commandling Zaldark.

Blet then asked with a puzzled look on his face, "But what could be gained from doing such a thing?"

"It would seem that the intruders have decided that whatever it is they want to do, they want to do without the worry of interference. I am not a knowledge seeker, but even I would think that anything that is on the main world would have difficulty in surviving for very long," answered Zaldark.

"But there are only simple creatures and vegetation living there," said Blet, having difficulty in understanding why someone would do such a thing.

"Yes, Overbeing," said Zaldark, "we know this to be, but the intruders may not, and if they covered the world in a dust cloud, it is obviously their plan to destroy all life forms and therefore any chance of retaliation."

"But why destroy all life on the world?" asked Blet.

Commandling Zaldark replied, "If you wish to destroy your enemy in a crowd and you cannot see him, then by destroying the crowd, you will surely succeed."

"So you are saying, that to avoid retaliation for their actions, the intruders have tried to destroy every

living thing on the world," said Blet, in absolute stunned horror at the thought.

"That would appear to be what has happened," said Zaldark.

"What could be of such great value that these monsters feel that they can cause such destruction to achieve whatever it is that they set out to do?" asked Blet with an increasing sense of loathing towards the creatures that can obviously place such little significance on living things.

"Perhaps it is that they wish to colonize this world as well," said Zaldark, "and by eliminating everything on it, they can do so without ever having to worry about an uprising."

"Or, maybe it is not the large world that they are interested in," said Krerbnot.

"What do you mean?" asked Blet.

"Remember, this small world would have but one use, and that is mineral excavation," explained Krerbnot. Could it be that the intruders are only interested in mining this world?"

"Maybe that is why they now circle the main world—to make sure that nothing is able to stop them, said Zaldark.

"This is indeed disturbing. To think that some creatures value artificial mineral wealth over living beings," said Blet.

Maintainer Zeral, who had been sitting quietly to one side, then decided to speak

"I would think," he said, "that a craft needed to carry out such a task would have to be three or four times as large as our own. What would happen if it were to locate us?"

"The chances of that happening are very slim, as Technician Zetkr has already pointed out," said Zaldark.

"We will not know any more, until we have actually seen this craft," said Krerbnot. "Then, we will speak with the sayers, to see what is the best path forward, and if the Great Protector is merciful, that path shall be the correct one."

WHAT NEXT?

J ulie pushed her chair back away from the desk and stretched out as much as she could whilst still sitting. After a few seconds, she relaxed again. Then, she thought that she would take a little break, and what better way to do that than listen to some music?

She reached into a small bag that she had sitting on the floor below her desk, retrieved a cubed object that was similar in size to a tea cup, and placed it on the desk in front of her.

Then, into a slot on the top, she placed a small square disc about the size of a thumbnail.

When she next pressed a button beside the disk, a small holographic image appeared above the cube to a height of approximately six inches, and the room started to fill with the sounds of Richard Clapton's song, "Capricorn Dancer".

Looking out at the stars whilst listening to the song relaxed her so much that she was given a start from a voice behind her that said, "That's nice."

Turning around, she saw Gary standing a few metres away.

"Sorry, I didn't mean to startle you," he said, "it's just that I could not sleep so I decided to go for a stroll. Then, I heard your music and thought I would come and check it out. I hope I am not intruding."

"No, it's fine," Julie replied. "It's just that this song relaxes me so much you could probably have blown my chair up, and I might not have noticed."

"Hmm," said Gary, "that is pretty relaxed."

"Yes, it is part of my grandfather's old music collection that I had hollodized," said Julie. "So, I don't know if it is the music or the memories that I have of listening to it with my grandfather when we would visit that relaxes me. I just know it does."

"I can't say that I listen to a lot of music," said Gary, almost apologetically. "I think I was born with two left ears."

"That is a serious affliction," said Julie smiling.

"Yes," said Gary, "but the doctors have all said that I should survive, I just shouldn't try to sing."

Julie just looked at him with a crooked smile and did not say anything.

"Anyway, why have you still got your nose to the grindstone?" asked Gary.

Julie could not help but laugh when she heard Gary use that term.

"I'm sorry," she said. "It's just that I can still remember when my grandfather would use that same phrase."

"So what are you trying to say, that I am so old that I remind you of your grandfather?" said Gary with a look of feigned indignation on his face.

"No, not at all," replied Julie. "It's just that it is not a term you hear very often these days."

"All right, I will forgive you this time," said Gary, "but you still have not said why you are still working when you are supposed to be resting."

"Like you, I could not really sleep, and I am still trying to figure out that anomaly. Although we have no record on file of it being there, and long range tests tell me it is not there, I can see from the data that I have collected that it is there," said Julie.

"What do you mean when you say tests say it is not there?" asked Gary with a puzzled look on his face.

"Well," said Julie, as she started to explain herself, "when we want to check the distance of something that is an extremely long way away, we can fire a modified laser beam at it and check the signal when it reaches its target.

"This one though, does not stop the laser, and it is like firing into a bottomless pit," she added, hoping Gary would understand.

"Could it be something like a cloud and the laser is passing right through it?" asked Gary, trying is best to help by asking a question about one of the few things that he knew to exist in deep space.

"No, I had thought of that," said Julie, "but you do not get clouds that form so small because it would appear from preliminary results that it could be as little as ten kilometres across."

"Also," she added, "clouds are not usually a uniform shape because they are a freely moving mass of gas and dust, but even then you would get some feedback. And the fact that the solar system is where it is in 65 million years gives us a fair indication that it is not a black hole."

"Well, that's reassuring," said Gary.

"Yes, indeed, and summing up so far, I can't tell you what it is, but I am starting to figure out what it is not," she said with the hint a smile on her face.

"Right, so if it's just a process of elimination, I'll just keep saying random objects until you say yes, and we will have our answer," said Gary, watching Julie's grin get broader.

"OK," answered Julie, "but to speed up the process, I will also eliminate elephant, Oldsmobile, and fish tank."

"Oh man, they were going to be my first guesses," said Gary.

"Sorry, I guess it's back to the drawing board then," Julie replied.

"What are you two doing up?"

They both turned to see Dr Western entering the room.

"Sorry, Doc. Couldn't sleep, so I thought that I would go for a stroll and try again later," said Gary.

"I don't want to sound like the grumpy parent," said Raul, "but please do, because we must regulate our sleep patterns if we don't want to all end up being so tired that mistakes start to happen."

Feeling a little like a naughty schoolboy, Gary said, "You're right, Doc. I'd better go and hit the sack."

"I'll see you both later," he added as he exited towards the sleeping quarters.

"I seem to recall that you are rostered for a rest period as well," said Raul, as he turned back to face Julie after watching Gary depart.

"Yes," she replied, "it's just that I am becoming so engrossed with this anomaly that I feel I have to study it all the time, or it might disappear just as I am ready to find out what it is."

"That is all good and well," said Raul, "but remember, do not become so obsessed that you neglect all other things. And also, remember the more rested you are, the easier things seem. I would be very surprised if the thing that you are studying is not still there when you wake up."

"Obviously you are right," conceded Julie, feeling a little flat after his comments. "I'll just make a few more short notes and head off."

"Please, do not think I am criticizing your work ethic. I just think that in our current environment rest is best," said Raul, noticing Julie's forlorn look.

Julie responded, "Again, you are right. I think I am just starting to feel a little tired, so now is probably a good time to try to get some sleep."

"Good," said Raul, "and when you wake, I will even make you a cup of tea."

"And don't think that I will not hold you to that," said Julie with a smile as she got to her feet after shutting her computer down and picking up the bag from below her desk and started heading towards the sleeping quarters.

"OK," said Raul, "I'll get it as soon as you start your next shift."

"Very well," said Julie over her shoulder. "I will see you then."

"Good night," said Raul, which seemed a little strange, as they were currently on the same side of the planet as the sun, but he knew it was just a reflexive response towards someone who was about to retire.

After she had departed, Raul turned and headed towards the control room to see how Tony was getting on.

"How are things going?" he asked, after he had entered the room and saw Tony busily typing into the main computer console.

"Dr Western," said Tony, looking up from his current task, "just checking that our speed and current course are still right."

"And is everything all right?" asked Raul.

"Yeah, I'm just making the slightest adjustment, more out of wanting something to do rather than necessity," replied Tony.

"Yes, well, a slight adjustment now may save a major adjustment later," said Raul, trying to make it sound as though no one action taken is less important than another.

"So I suppose we micromanage our way through this until something happens," said Tony.

"Well, that is one way of looking at it," replied Raul, "but remember, we are all in this together and you, like the others, are part of a team. The more we work together, the better our chances are."

"You're right," said Tony, as he sat back in his chair and began to stare out of the window towards the Moon. "It's just that I don't like sitting around not being able to do what I was trained to do."

"Yes, that is frustrating, but we cannot lose focus, because if we are not working together, nothing will be achieved," said Raul, trying his best to reassure Tony.

"You needn't worry, Dr Western," said Tony, "I am definitely a member of the team, and if—"

Tony paused and then said, "What was that?"

"What was what?" asked Raul.

"It was like a flash right next to the Moon," said Tony, as he leaned forward in his seat, trying to give himself a better view.

"What do you mean? Like an explosion?" asked Raul, as he tried to see if he could notice anything in the general direction that Tony was looking.

"No, it was like when you are driving along a road and the sun briefly reflects on an object at the right angle so as to make it flash momentarily as you go past it," said Tony, as he tried to explain what he saw.

After a few moments of looking, Raul said, "I can't say that I see anything out of the ordinary."

"I am positive that I saw something," said Tony, hoping to catch another glimpse, maybe to prove more to himself than Dr Western that he was not starting to imagine things.

"I am not saying you didn't, I am just saying it could have been a trick of the light or a meteorite crashing into the Moon," said Raul, "because, I do not think we were close enough to any satellites to drag them back with us through time, even if we could for that matter."

"Yes, well, up until the time that we arrived here, I would have thought that any sort of time travel was not possible," replied Tony.

"Granted that is true, but like I said, there does not appear to be anything out of the ordinary out there," said Raul.

After a few more seconds, Tony sat back in his seat and said, "You're right. It must have been a trick of the light."

"Right then," said Raul. "I might check the readouts for the core, then go and do a physical check to make sure everything is still correlated."

"OK, and I will make a few more minor adjustments, then maybe try some small course alterations, just to make sure we can still steer this thing if need be," replied Tony.

"You don't need Gary to help you with that?" asked Raul.

"Not for the small changes I want to try," answered Tony.

"OK, I will leave you with it then," said Raul, as he headed over to check his readouts.

"Thanks, and I will try not to crash into any strange lights I might see," said Tony, still looking out of the window.

"That would be good," said Raul with the hint of a smile on his face and realizing that Gary's sense of humour, like a virulent flu, was starting to infect others.

THE FACTS

"Mrs Western?" inquired Inspector Watts, as he held out his ID so that the woman opening the door could see it.

"No, I am her sister, Stephanie Joseph. Can I help you?" came the reply.

"Yes, I am Inspector Watts and this is Deputy Assistant Neville," he said, gesturing to his partner before turning back to face Ms Joseph.

"We're from IMPol, and we are investigating the Moonshaker incident, and I was hoping that we might be able to have a chat with Mrs Western," said the inspector, trying his best not to sound too obtrusive.

"I am sorry," said Stephanie in a calm but firm voice, "but she is still very upset, and the best thing she can do now is rest. When she is feeling up to it, I will tell her you called, and then—"

"Who is it Steph? Is that the police? Have they found her? What's happening?" came an animated voice from another room.

"It's all right, Tan," said Stephanie, calling her sister by her pet name that she had used since childhood. "It's the army police just wanting to ask some questions about what happened."

"I told them they can come back later," stated Stephanie, feeling very protective of her younger sister.

"No, don't be silly," replied Tania, walking up behind her sister. "They're here now. They may as well come in, and hopefully they can help find Ellie."

"I am just thinking of you, Tan," said Stephanie, feeling a little put out over the fact that her sister would not take her advice. "You know the best thing for you now is rest. The last thing I want is for you to get sick, and then you won't be any good to anyone."

"Steph, please. I am not ten years old anymore," said Tania in exasperation of the fact that she felt that her sister was trying to smother her.

"Well, excuse me for trying to help," said Stephanie before she turned and walked down the hallway, before disappearing into the kitchen.

"Oh, don't mind her. Please come in," said Tania.

She gestured for the two men to enter as they looked uncertainly at each other.

"Thank you," said the inspector as they entered and were then guided into the living room.

"So, have you found out anything about Ellie?" asked Tania, eager for any news about her stepdaughter.

"I'm sorry, Ma'am. We are actually investigating the incident with the Moonshaker project, and I am afraid we do not know anything about your daughter," said the inspector, clarifying why they were there and at the same time, trying not to sound too distant to Tania's fears for her daughter.

"But Steph said you were the police," said Tania with a look of puzzlement on her face.

"That is correct, Ma'am, but we are with the military police, and if there is a matter you wish to discuss pertaining to your daughter then that is a civil matter and you need to discuss it with the local authorities," replied the inspector, trying desperately to sound helpful and not to sound too cold.

"I'm sorry," said Tania as she struggled to keep her composure. "It's like I do not know what is happening and why everything is going so wrong."

"I am sure that the relevant authorities are doing all they can, Mam," said Inspector Watts, trying to reassure her.

"Of course you are right," said Tania, calming slightly, "but it is not like her to just go somewhere and not let anyone know."

"Actually, I have a friend in the missing persons bureau who may be able to help," said Deputy Neville, hoping to put Mrs Western a little more at ease.

"Oh please, I would be very grateful if he could," said Tania with an almost pleading look in her eyes.

"I will contact him as soon as we leave," said Deputy Neville, giving her what he thought was a reassuring smile.

"Thank you," said Tania, feeling a little better knowing that others were actually concerned for Ellie's safety as well.

"Now then, why are you investigating the accident?" asked Tania uncertainly. "I thought it was a malfunction that caused it."

Inspector Watts looked at Deputy Neville and was momentarily unsure of how to proceed, as he had been led to believe that Mrs Western had been told of the apparent sabotage.

"I am sorry," said the inspector. "I thought that you had been notified of the latest information."

"Information pertaining to what?" asked Tania, feeling like all her news of late had been bad, and now it did not seem as though it was going to get better.

"Well, Ma'am," said the inspector, deciding that the best route was straight ahead, "our latest intelligence is leading us to believe that it was not so much an accident as it was more than likely sabotage."

Upon hearing this, Tania just went numb, and she sat in silence for a few seconds, trying to gather her thoughts whilst an almost overwhelming sense of emotion swept over her.

She felt as though she wanted to cry and scream and ask why and who and accuse people and ask how it could have happened and what about security. Eventually, she just placed her head in her hands and did something that she had not done since the accident—she began to sob.

Upon hearing her sister crying, Stephanie entered the room, looking like a mother about to scold her children.

"I told you she needed rest," she said berating the inspector.

"I'm truly sorry, Ma'am. It was not my intention to upset anyone," said the inspector apologetically.

"If you wish, we will take our leave."

"No, it's all right," said Tania, trying to compose herself. "I just need a minute."

"Tan, I really think you should rest," said Stephanie in what she thought was an authoritative tone.

"Steph, really, I will be fine. I think I just needed to get that out of my system," replied Tania, finally getting herself under control.

"If you want, we can come back another time when you are feeling better," said the inspector.

"No, really, I will be fine," said Tania. "It was just a bit of a shock to hear, but like I said, I think I just needed to get it out of my system."

"Please, Steph. I will be fine," she said as her sister looked at her as if she was the only one capable of making the right decisions on all things of any importance.

After a few seconds, Stephanie replied, "Very well, but I will be close by if you need me."

Then she slowly turned and walked through the door leading back into the kitchen.

After watching Stephanie leave the room, Tania turned her attention back to the two men.

"Now, you said it could have been sabotage. What? Why? Who . . . ?" she stammered, obviously still feeling a little flustered over the latest revelation.

"It's all right, Ma'am," said the inspector, trying to put Tania at ease. "We think it could have been something placed on the impulse gun that reacted when it was fired that actually caused the explosion."

"Do you know who it was that could have done this?" asked Tania starting to think more clearly.

"That is what we are currently trying to find out," answered the inspector.

"I would think you could start with that horrid Graeme Rogerson," Tania said without trying to mask the contempt in her voice.

"Well, Ma'am, that is why we need to gather as much information as we can so that the people who are responsible will be held accountable," said the inspector.

"And with that, we must make sure we are dealing with facts and not emotions," he added. "So please, try to answer questions with what you know to have happened and not what you think someone may have done."

"Yes, of course. I will do my best," said Tania, feeling as though she had just been chided by a teacher for misspelling a word.

"Do you recall if anyone ever threatened yourself or Dr Western?" asked the inspector.

"Not that I remember, and Raul never said anything," answered Tania.

"Did he ever mention anything that happened on site that did not seem to be as it should?" asked the inspector.

"What do you mean?" asked Tania.

"For example, did someone say something that did not seem right or maybe an unexplained delivery," said the inspector.

"Not really," said Tania, "although he did mention, that he wondered how they would be able to lift off if people kept doing what it was that they were doing."

"What did he mean by that?" asked the inspector.

"Well, it's just that he was saying with weight restrictions being so regimented, he was a little miffed at the way some were bringing in more and more crates of equipment," explained Tania.

"What sort of equipment?" asked Inspector Watts.

"He couldn't really say," answered Tania, "as they were in sealed crates."

"But," she continued, "he knew that it was not really a problem because all deliveries would have to be authorized and weights measured."

"Did he say who it as that these deliveries were for?" asked Deputy Neville.

"Yes, he said it was mainly Tony and Dr Peterson. He also said he could understand Tony wanting specialized equipment to help in navigation and aid in being able to pilot the craft, but he could not understand why Dr Peterson would need so much extra. He thought that the computing system that was installed was by far the best you could get, and obviously, the software was not something that was available to the general public."

"Did he ever say that Tony or Dr Peterson brought any unauthorized personnel onto the base?" asked the inspector.

"Not that I recall," said Tania, "but then again, he did say that Dr Peterson was a very quiet person, almost to the point of being reclusive, and did not really interact with the others."

"Did Dr Western say if he was concerned by this?" asked Deputy Neville.

"No," Tania replied, "because he knew that Dr Peterson's credentials were impeccable, and that all the mathematicians he knew were fairly idiosyncratic."

Inspector Watts gave a slight chuckle and said, "Yes, I actually have a couple of friends in that field, and to say they are idiosyncratic is being polite."

"Did he ever say anything about the others?" the inspectors asked.

"Like what?" asked Tania.

"For example, how they were acting, who they were meeting—just little things like that," said the inspector.

"Well, he has known Gary since the accident and has built up a relationship of friendship and respect over the last fourteen years. I think he may have been taken by the fact that Dr Anders has so much acclaim for achieving what she has at such a young age, and yet, whenever he spoke to her, he said she seemed to be so grounded and just such a pleasant person."

"So he ever voiced any concern over the crew?" asked the inspector.

"No, but as you can imagine, he was busy with his own work, and there were others that would have been in charge of security," Tania replied.

"Yes, of course," said the inspector getting to his feet.

"I think we have taken up enough of your time, and I also hope that we did not intrude or that we upset you too much."

"No, really, I am fine. But thank you for your concern," replied Tania

"And please, if you remember anything, no matter how insignificant it may seem, do not hesitate to call," said the inspector holding out a card with his details on it for Tania to take.

"Thank you," said Tania as she stood to escort the two men out of the house.

"Once again, thank you for your time, and I hope everything works out with your daughter," said the inspector as he and Deputy Neville stood on the porch, about to take their leave.

"Thank you," was all Tania could say as she watched the two men turn and walk towards their car.

As they entered the car, both men turned and waved to the forlorn figure of the lone woman standing in the doorway, and Deputy Neville said, "Man, I hope Stewart can help."

Being the head of missing person's bureau, Stewart Jones was probably the best hope they had of finding Mrs Western's daughter, but as he had often told Deputy Neville, less than 10 per cent of missing people, are located.

Neville just hoped that Ellie would be in that group.

"Yes, I think any good news that woman got would be a welcome relief," said Inspector Watts as he pulled the car away from the curb.

"So what was the accident that she was referring to?" Deputy Neville asked his superior.

Concentrating on the road ahead, the inspector answered.

"As Mrs Western said, it was fourteen years ago, and Dr Western's first wife had just dropped their daughter at the daycare centre before heading off to work.

"Unfortunately for her, Scott White was also on the road that morning, but unlike her, White had not been to bed the previous night. He had been laid off from work the day before, and after trying to drown his sorrows all night, decided that it would be a good idea if he finally drove home to get some sleep. As Dr Western's wife was proceeding through a green set of traffic lights, White arrived, already passed out, coming from the side street. She did not stand a chance," concluded the inspector.

"I think I might remember something about that," said Deputy Neville. "Wasn't he the guy that tried to sue the bar for serving him so much alcohol, and therefore, they were responsible?"

"Yeah, that was him," said the inspector, "but the prosecutors successfully argued that he was the one that made the choice to drink and as he had said that he was going to go outside and hail a cab. No one knew his real intention was to try and drive home."

"So, he lost his job, took a life, and is currently serving twenty-four years for vehicular manslaughter," said the inspector.

"What about that Gary fellow?" the deputy then asked.

"Gary Roebottom was the patrolman on duty that morning and first on the scene," said the inspector.

"He was also the one tasked with telling Dr Western about the accident."

"Man, that is a job I have not had nor ever want," said Deputy Neville.

"No, it is not one you ever forget in a hurry," said the inspector, still concentrating on the road ahead, as they continued their drive.

PLAN "B"

As General Fredrickson and his aide approached the conference room, he was still going over in his mind about what had happened since the explosion, information he had been given about the ongoing investigation, and possible contingency plans, because he knew he had to convince the World Council that he was still the best person to bring a solution to the events that had unfolded.

When he entered he could see that many of the seats had already been filled by other people who had been invited because they had a vested interest in the outcome of this meeting

Once they had made their way to the front table that had been set up so that the World Council could question them on how the investigation was proceeding, a side door opened, and the League of Seven entered and took their place, according to seniority, behind the bench that had been set up at the head of the room.

The central position was taken by Councillor Sebastian Leparge, who was three months into his twelve month term as head of the World Council. The general knew that he had to convince Leparge to get this project back up and running within the next nine months; otherwise, the general would have to start to deal with the new head councillor when the head councillor would resign and a new councillor would be elected to the League of Seven.

When all seven councillors had taken their seats, with Stefan Billotson being the last to take a seat as he was the newest member of the League of Seven, General Fredrickson knew that the questions were not far away.

"General Fredrickson," said Councillor Leparge, "I hope you are well."

The general knew that the statement was posed in reference to him letting himself get more than a little run down, due to trying to shoulder the greater bulk of the work load.

"Yes, thank you, Councillor. I have heeded the words of my physician and find myself delegating a little more, replied the general.

"That is indeed good news," said the councillor, "for we at the council know the important contribution you make towards this project."

Upon hearing this, the general's shoulders went back and his back seemed to straighten ever so slightly.

"Thank you for your kind words, Councillor," said the general.

"Of course, General," replied Councillor Leparge. "Now, what news can you give us about proceedings thus far."

The general took a few seconds to arrange the paperwork that his aide had handed him before answering.

"The man I have heading the investigation from the military prospective is Chief Investigator Major Peter Watts, and in his report last night, he said that although he still was not sure who placed the explosives, he was confident that he was going to be able to find out. Once he has done that, he said that it would only be a matter of time before he found the supply route and all those involved," said the general.

"That is good, General, but did he give a time frame?"

This time the question was asked by Theobold Weddell, the councillor set to replace Councillor Leparge when he retired

"As you can well imagine, Councillor, an investigation of this nature is rather complex, and to place a definitive time frame on it, would be extremely difficult," answered the general.

"However, having said that, Major Watts did say that he thought it would be sooner rather than later," he added.

"A little ambiguous, General, but still if the major feels he is making steady progress, then that is probably all we can hope for, for now," said Councillor Leparge.

"So tell us, General, what does that then mean in relation to the mission?"

It was third in line of the council, Councillor Able Krandowsky who asked the question.

"It has obviously stalled the project for the time being, but I truly believe that it was the correct path that we were taking, and I also think that we need to keep working on the project, because it is easier to keep something going than to stop and restart it," said the general.

"So are you saying we should build another Moonshaker satellite?" asked Councillor Leparge.

"Yes, that is what I am saying," said the general, making sure that this answer had no ambiguity.

"This will still be possible without Dr Western?" asked Councillor Weddell.

"Although Dr Western is not here, we have all of his information pertaining to the project, as well as all the people who worked on the first satellite. The lessons learned from the first build have taught us so much, that yes, it most certainly is possible," said the general with as much confidence as he could exude.

"And what of security?" asked Councillor Leparge. "Will you be able to guarantee the safety of the project?"

"As I have said, lessons learned from the first build have taught us a great deal, not leastwise about our security protocols," replied the general.

"And with that," he continued, "an overhaul of procedures is taking place. So I have complete confidence that the project would be secure."

"General Fredrickson," said Councillor Krandowsky, "the last project took just under five years. How long do you envisage it would take to complete another satellite?"

"Well," said the general, knowing that this would not be seen as positive news, "although we have Dr Western's notes and a now-experienced build team, without Dr Western actually being here it could take seven to ten years before we are ready to launch."

"And what would the cost of this project be?" asked Councillor Luke Matsumoto, who, as fifth in line within the council, was in charge of financial matters.

"Because a lot of the equipment that was used in the construction phase has not yet been decommissioned, a considerable saving will be able to be made in that area," said the general, hoping to start with something positive before trying to ease into a final cost without too much of a shock.

"However," he added, "having said that, as you can imagine, over time costs rise and the last five years are no exception to that rule."

"Of course, General, that is understood, but do you have an actual cost?" asked Councillor Matsumoto.

"The latest projected figure puts the cost at just over double the last mission," the general replied.

After a few seconds, Councillor Leparge said, "That is quite a considerable sum, General."

"That it is, Councillor, but the cost of not doing anything would make this seem an insignificant amount," replied the general.

"Please do not think that we are contemplating doing nothing, General," said Councillor Leparge, with a hint of annoyance in his voice for thinking the general would suggest such a thing. "I am saying that the amount of money you are suggesting will not come easily, as there are many other projects of great importance that are in urgent need of funding."

"So," he added, "we need to make sure that we can solve one problem without creating another."

"Of course, Councillor. I meant no disrespect," was the general's apologetic reply.

"Now then," continued Councillor Leparge, "the first Moonshaker program was chosen because at the time, although it was more expensive than alternate plans, the cost for the expected result made it the most logical choice. So, in light of your statement about the project being more than double the cost, would an alternate method be a more prudent choice?"

"I believe the Moonshaker project is still our best and surest method of correcting the problem," the general said.

"Could you explain to us why you are so certain of this, General?" said Councillor Weddell.

"The first alternate plan of placing propulsion engines on a strategically located area of the Moon and continually running them to gently push the Moon back into its correct orbit would require a fleet of rockets to supply the fuel needed. And we would have to hope that none of the engines failed, because then we would have to interrupt the fuel supply in order to carry out repairs," explained the general.

"The second alternate plan, which was to launch nuclear-loaded rockets to explode at a predetermined distance from the surface so as to jolt it back into orbit, is fraught with so much danger from the launch already being one of the most dangerous stages of any flight to now having the capability of becoming a time for a potentially catastrophic nuclear disaster, to the fact that if the explosion was to take place at the wrong altitude, it would do nothing but damage the surface if it were too close, or nothing at all, if it were too far away."

"Also," he continued, "the resources needed to be continuously manufacturing launch vehicles would eventually make them both uneconomical."

"And these are still the only alternate ideas?" asked Councillor Leparge.

"When it was decided that something needed to be done, there were numerous ideas discussed, but these were the only three that were seriously considered," replied the general.

"Would it be more prudent of us if we were to wait for a period of time, say six months, to see if there was someone that may come up with another idea?" asked Councillor Krandowsky.

"I truly believe, as I have said before," replied the general, "that the Moonshaker project is still our best option, and the longer we delay, the higher the costs are going to be."

"Well, thank you, General," said Councillor Leparge. "I think what we should do now, is retire to consider our next course of action, and we will reconvene here again in two weeks to discuss our findings."

"Very good, Councillor. I look forward to that meeting," said the general as he then watched the councillors all stand and exit through the same door that they had entered earlier.

"Well, how do you think that went?" asked the general's aide.

"I guess we will find out in two weeks," replied the general, wondering if there was anything else that he could have said that would have made a difference and then realizing that for the time being it was out of his hands.

FIRST SIGHT

"Controller Krerbnot, the craft is coming into view," said Technician Zetkr.

"Put the images on the main viewing screen," said Krerbnot.

"Maintainer Zeral, what do you make of this?" he then asked as the images were being displayed.

"I would think it does not appear to be as large as we thought," Zeral answered.

"What would that then tell us?" asked Krerbnot.

"That maybe this is not a vessel that would be used for excavation," replied Zeral.

Overbeing Blet then asked, "If this is not a craft for mineral excavation, what would its purpose be?"

Commandling Zaldark answered, "It would appear that if its mission is not one of mineral exploration, then it would most likely be to secure the area."

"How so?" asked Blet.

"Well, once they have secured the main world and can see that there will be no resistance, they will then be free to explore and then report on their findings of the mineral world."

"So, are you saying that this is an advance mission?" asked Blet.

"I believe so," said Zaldark, "and, I think that once they have made sure they have eliminated all threats to themselves, they will set out for a closer look at their prize. I also believe that because of what they have done to the main world, if we are discovered, they will see us as a threat and take steps to eliminate us."

"Controller Krerbnot, you said before that we had a weapons array that we could use to defend ourselves against many things, would it be effective against a craft of this size?" asked Blet.

"I have no doubt that it would, but we must also be wary of the fact that because they have the capability to destroy a world, we may not be much of a problem to them if they are able to attack us first," Krerbnot replied.

"So what do you suggest as a course of action?" was Blet's next question.

Zaldark answered, "At this stage, I would say that we should observe as much as we can, and once they know they have secured the main world and start to move to investigate their options for the excavation, that is when we must be ready to act."

"So, if the craft does start to move towards us, then we will be certain that its purpose is mineral exploration?" asked Blet.

"Yes, I think then there would be no doubting their intention," Zaldark replied.

"And if the craft does not move out of its orbit, what then do we think of its actions?" asked Blet.

"I could think of no other reason as to why they would cause so much destruction," Zaldark replied, "and with that, I am certain that they will move to this small world."

"Then when they do, we must make sure that we are ready," said Blet.

"With the element of surprise, I think we will be more than ready," said Zaldark, with a look of almost expectant anticipation of an upcoming battle.

ALTERNATIVES

"Ah, Dr Western, just the person I wished to speak to," said Dr Peterson as he walked towards Raul, who had just finished checking the core drive, again.

"Dr Peterson, how can I help you?" asked Raul.

"I have some news that I think will please you very much," said Dr Peterson, trying very hard to build the excitement over what he thought would be a ground-breaking revelation.

"Well, I am always ready to hear good news," said Raul. "What is it that you have to tell me?"

"I may have found a way back," said Dr Peterson, unable to contain himself.

The statement took Raul totally by surprise, and it was a few seconds before he could gather his thoughts.

"Are you sure?" he was eventually able to ask.

"I have done a little work on my preliminary findings, but I think my results could be positive," answered Dr Peterson.

"Very well," said Raul, "could you give me an outline of your findings?"

"Of course, of course," said Dr Peterson.

"I first had to try and figure out the exact circumstances that brought us here, and although there was the explosion, I thought that the explosion itself would not be able to create the circumstances necessary to bring about the result. So, I started to look elsewhere, and that was when I figured that it was a by-product of the explosion that was the main contributing factor."

"Go on," said Raul.

"Heat," said Dr Peterson.

Raul said nothing. He knew that Dr Peterson would explain further.

"Now," continued Dr Peterson, "heat in itself would not be enough to cause time travel, obviously, otherwise you would have stars jumping from one time period to another all over the universe. But intense heat in a very small area, whilst in an extremely cold environment, which is what would have happened when the impulse gun was fired and the tiles exploded, should, theoretically, be enough to create such a temperature differentiation as to create a hole in the fabric of space and therefore allow passage to another time zone."

"I see," said Raul. "Do you have any idea of the amount of heat that would be required?"

"After running some simulations, I figure it would have to be just above the heat generated in the centre of the sun," was the reply.

"Indeed," said Raul, after a moment or two of silence. "So, are you suggesting that we have to travel to the centre of the sun in order to get back?"

"No, of course not—as we both know, that would be impossible," Dr Peterson replied, "but if we got close enough so that the temperature would be able to be raised to the required amount when the impulse gun was fired, it could work."

"'Could work' is not a very confident statement," said Raul.

"Yes, well, there is the variable of the external temperature," said Dr Peterson. "I mean, where we were when the explosion occurred the outside temperature was below minus 200 degrees Celsius, so the contrast when it happened would have been severe, like piercing a thin piece of plastic with a red-hot wire. The problem being, that the closer to the sun you get, the higher the outside temperature becomes, and it would be more difficult to obtain the temperature difference needed."

"So, how would you think that this could be made to work?" Raul asked, not totally abandoning the idea.

"We would have to see if we have a recording of the temperature that was reached during the explosion to check and see if my calculations are correct," said Dr Peterson. "Next, we would have to fire the impulse gun at differing levels to find out what temperatures are being generated. Then, it would just be a matter of being at the right distance from the sun so that when we fire the impulse gun at the right setting we would be able to create enough heat as to get the temperature differentiation needed to recreate the hole in the space-time continuum and we could travel through."

"That is indeed an interesting theory," said Raul, "but there are quite a few variables. First, if we are not close enough, nothing may happen; then, if we are too close, it could be catastrophic. Then there is the matter of the external temperature.

"Obviously, the higher the temperature of our surroundings, the higher the temperature that would have to be created, and this craft was not really designed to withstand temperatures of the magnitude that you are suggesting."

"And," he added, "even if it does work, who is to say that we would end up from whence we came."

"Yes, they are valid points," responded Dr Peterson, "but the fact that we are here shows us that this craft can withstand the great temperatures needed for such a venture. And as for the fact that we may not go back to our own time, I mean, surely we cannot stay here indefinitely."

Dr Western replied, "It is true that the craft did survive the first blast, but do not forget, by your own findings, due to the external temperature of our current location the temperature variation would have been contained to a very small area, and we would have been shielded from it by the impulse gun itself. You are right in the fact that we will not be able to stay here indefinitely, but the fact that we have no idea of where we would end up, even if it did work, does not really fill me with confidence either.

"But I think you are right in the fact that we should measure the temperatures created when the impulse gun is fired, because I also think that you have come up with a very interesting theory," he concluded.

"Yes," said Dr Peterson with a sigh, "having you say it back to me like that does tend to make me feel a little less enthusiastic than I was when I first came up with the idea. It's just that I have a feeling that I am not really contributing. So when I came upon this theory, I wanted to believe it so much that I didn't really look at it as objectively as maybe I should have."

Raul looked at him squarely and said, "Dr Peterson, since the explosion, some of the roles we were allocated have changed drastically—not the least of which was yours. For now, no longer are you expected to calculate distance, power, angle, and thrust so that we may be able to push the Moon back into its correct orbit, but we have asked you to redefine the laws of physics to come up with a solution to a problem that we have been told is impossible. The fact that you have tells me that not only are you contributing, you are doing so with spectacular success."

"Oh, I think spectacular success may be a little strong," said Dr Peterson, feeling modest but at the same time feeling proud of the praise given him by a peer.

"Well, even though I found flaws in the idea does not mean that it is not a sound theory," said Raul.

"Maybe it is just that you need more time to work on some of your calculations," he added.

"And it would appear that time is something that we have an abundance of," said Dr Peterson.

"Yes," replied Raul. "So please, may I suggest that you do not use the time feeling as though you are not contributing but use it to continue with the work you are already doing. Who knows, you just may be able to make that final breakthrough."

"Thank you for your confidence in me, Dr Western. I shall return to my task with renewed vigour," said Dr Peterson.

"I am glad to hear it," said Raul.

Now, feeling much better about himself, Dr Peterson thought he should continue the conversation.

"So, how is Dr Anders getting on with her work?" he asked.

"She has become so engrossed with that anomaly she has found that it is actually a task to get her to rest," Raul answered.

"Maybe I could offer to help her," said Dr Peterson.

"That would be up to her of course," said Raul, "but I do not think that she would pass up the opportunity for external input."

"Then I shall speak to her about it," said Dr Peterson, "but now, if you will excuse me, I think I will take some of Gary's advice."

Raul turned to look directly at Dr Peterson.

Then, with a curious look on his face he asked, "What advice would that be?"

"He said that I should not be afraid to stop every now and then and have a cup of coffee," answered Dr Peterson.

Raul then said with a slight grin on his face, "That would probably not be the worst advice Gary has ever offered."

Unsure on how to respond to this last statement, Dr Peterson just said, "Indeed," and then left to go and make his coffee, leaving Raul to reminisce about some of the things that Gary had tried to convince Ellie were true.

IN CHARGE

"Mr Rogerson, so glad you could see us at such short notice," said Inspector Watts, as he and Deputy Neville were being ushered to chairs on one side of a grand desk whilst Graeme Rogerson took his place in a large leather chair on the other side.

The image that both men had of Graeme Rogerson was the image that they had seen on hollovision, and that was of a large, confident person who created an atmosphere wherever he went.

They could see that he seemed confident, but he was far from being a large man and, as for projecting an atmosphere, neither of them could really feel it.

"Of course, Inspector," said Rogerson, "I am only too glad to help."

"I am happy to hear that," said the inspector. "I wonder, if you would not mind, if we could start by asking about some of the members in your organization."

"Well, I will answer as best as I can," said Rogerson, "but please remember that everyone has a right to privacy, and I would not think that members of the AIL would be any different."

"Indeed," replied the inspector, "but the information we are after is not so much about private details but general matters."

"General matters? In what respect?" asked Rogerson.

"Oh, just little things, like something said in general conversation that may have seemed strange at the time or people you may not have recognized turning up to meetings," said the inspector, trying not to give too much away, as he could see that by asking questions Rogerson was trying to control the conversation.

"As you can imagine, Inspector, the number of members in our organization would make it extremely difficult to remember every conversation that I have had with them," said Rogerson.

"And as for seeing people who I did not recognize," he continued, "the fact that there are new members arriving all the time means that that is always going to be the case."

"So, you had no conversations that would have led you to believe that someone was planning to do something to the Moonshaker program?" asked the inspector.

"Obviously, the answer is no, Inspector. As I have already said to the police, although I do not condone the use of violence or the measures taken, I do respect the rights of people to demonstrate or show their disapproval to ideas they do not agree with," said Rogerson.

"So, you think it is all right to take five lives and destroy billions of dollars and five years of work that would have helped the planet, just because you do not agree with the idea?" asked Deputy Neville.

"Again the answer is no," said Rogerson, "for as I have just said, the use of violence is not the answer."

"So how would you have stopped the project?" asked the inspector.

"By the use of people power, Inspector," replied Rogerson.

"What? By preaching hatred towards those you oppose and then whipping up a bit of anti-government fervour by holding rallies with a large number of like-minded people?" asked Deputy Neville, realizing that the more he spoke to Rogerson, the less he liked him.

"No, Deputy," Rogerson said, putting emphasis on the title so that Deputy Neville knew that he thought of him as an underling.

"I would try to convince people that the ideas I had were the correct ones, and then, when I had garnered enough support, I would contact my local member, and show that not everyone was in support of certain decisions that had been made."

"Is this what you told Strand?" asked the inspector.

"I do not actually recall having a conversation with Mr Strand," replied Rogerson.

"So, he never contacted you in regard to this matter?" the inspector then asked.

"No," said Rogerson.

"For an organization that is so big you cannot remember every conversation, you seem very certain that this one did not take place," said Deputy Neville.

Rogerson gave the deputy a look of disdain before he answered.

"As I have continually said, Deputy, I do not believe violence is any sort of a solution. So, by not discussing it, you do not give people a platform to air their vitriolic views."

"Or maybe by not discussing it," replied the deputy, "you keep it out of public sight so that you are free to plot your 'revolutionary coup' without any interference."

Rogerson just looked at the deputy without saying anything, but his body language showed that he was becoming a little annoyed at the junior officer.

"Very well then, what can you tell us about Mr Strand?" asked the inspector, trying to regain control of the conversation,

"I do not recall a great deal that I could tell you," replied Rogerson.

"If you could try, it would be appreciated," said Deputy Neville with a slight tone of sarcasm in his voice.

The inspector gave his deputy a glance that let him know that he was not totally pleased, as he knew he needed Rogerson's help and purposefully goading him would not be the best way of obtaining it.

"There is not a great deal to remember about Strand," said Rogerson, "because he never seemed to do anything that would make you notice him."

"I mean," he continued, "I don't really recall a time when he would actively participate in any major discussions or put forward any ideas of possible action. He seemed to be content in just sitting quietly at meetings, taking everything in."

"Can you recall if he was at many meetings?" asked the inspector.

"Well, it was not as though I would be looking for him, but he was a recognizable face at most meetings," said Rogerson.

"Do you know if he was associating with anyone else in particular?" asked Deputy Neville, with a slightly more civil tone.

"I'm sorry," said Rogerson, "but who he was seeing is not information that I have readily available."

"So, you didn't notice if he was part of a group of people who always seemed to be together?" asked the inspector.

"Well, people would often congregate in groups after meetings, but as for knowing who was in what group, I am sorry, but that was something I did not take much notice of," replied Rogerson.

"Did anybody else ever talk of stronger actions that could be taken to further the cause of the league?" asked the inspector.

"Everyone has their own opinion, Inspector, but as I have said, a course of violence is not what I would see as being productive or, for that matter, the best way forward," said Rogerson.

"So, are you saying that not everyone within the organization agreed with your ideals?" asked Deputy Neville.

"I would love to be able to say they did," answered Rogerson, "but, as with any large organization, people are going to have differing opinions."

"I would see nothing sinister in that," he added. "I would see it as just a fact."

"Was there anyone in particular that thought strongly against your views?" asked the inspector.

"Obviously, there were some that did not agree with everything I said, but after we had discussed things, I was able to convince them that the broader plans that I had for the league, would be the most beneficial," said Rogerson.

"And what would those plans entail?" asked Deputy Neville.

"That we should try to convince as many people as we can that our views are correct, and that through logic and discussion we would be best able to show this rather than through violence and destruction," explained Rogerson.

"Do you mean to say, that others who did not agree with you were advocating the use of violent means?" asked Inspector Watts.

Rogerson started to move around in his seat a little more than he usually did before he answered.

"I could not say that the use of violence was their main priority, it is just that they were looking to become more proactive in the recruitment of new members, rather than just waiting for them to come to us."

"By proactive do you mean blowing up a space station and then seeing how many people applaud?" asked Deputy Neville.

"No, Deputy," replied Rogerson, starting to feel a little less assured, "I mean that they wanted to hold large mass rallies in public places, and I thought that rallies such as that, with sentiment running so high, could have the potential to become very nasty and would actually have an adverse effect on the popularity of the league."

"Would you be able to give us the names of these people?" asked the inspector.

"As I said before, Inspector, everyone has a right to privacy, and I would not like to think that someone was being persecuted merely because I mentioned their name." replied Rogerson.

"No one is going to be persecuted, Mr Rogerson," said the inspector. "I am merely trying to find out about the incident with the Moonshaker project, and anyone who may have information pertaining to this matter would be of great help to me."

"So if, as you say, you are only too glad to help, then I would appreciate it if you could give me the names of the people who you were speaking of."

"Then," he continued, "we can have a chat with them and hopefully they will be able to help us in our inquiries. If not, then our investigation may have to take a different direction."

After looking at the inspector and then Deputy Neville, Rogerson finally said, "Very well then—but just to let you know, I do not feel entirely comfortable with this."

"Mr Rogerson, please," said the inspector, "we are only interested in finding out what happened, and we are not going to be kicking in people's doors and sending them to the Chinese sulphur mines."

Now, even more unsure of what to think, as he was not totally sure if the inspector was joking or making a veiled threat, Rogerson began typing on his keyboard.

Then, he said, "There is a group of five, but the person who would seem to be most vocal is a man by the name of Joshua Grange. I am just getting his last known address."

"Thank you, Mr Rogerson," said the inspector, "that is very much appreciated."

Rogerson did not say anything; he just wrote down and then handed Grange's address to the inspector.

"Once again, thank you, Mr Rogerson," said the inspector getting to his feet, "but I feel we have taken up enough of your time. So if you will excuse us, I think we should take our leave, and please, do not hesitate to call if there is anything that you remember."

"Of course, Inspector," said Rogerson as he watched the two men leave his office.

Once they had departed, he picked up the phone, because he knew that there was someone he needed to call immediately.

WAITING

As Blet entered his living quarters, he saw Kretyabotkl busying herself by making sure the room was neat and orderly and therefore not cluttered and uncomfortable.

She looked up at him as he entered but did not say anything. For, even though theirs was a harmonious union, she still respected the fact that because of his position he should be the one to initiate a conversation.

"There are many I know, that would insist that this is work not befitting a senior sharebeing," he said in a not too serious tone.

"There are many I know that do not have a sharebeing that has such compassion as to allow his core unit to operate with such freedom," she replied.

"That is true," he said, "but then, not many have the sharebeings and younglings that the Great Protector has blessed me with."

This statement gladdened Kretyabotkl, and she gave him a hug, a form of affection rarely shown outside of one's abode.

Blet looked straight into her eyes and said, "You know that you are a great comfort to me," knowing that praise given can at times be worth more than units of wealth.

"It pleases me that you say this," replied Kretyabotkl, trying to reassure him, as she could see the worried look on his face.

Kretyabotkl knew that because of Blet's position for a sharebeing to ask questions without being prompted was not something that was really done, but she also knew that theirs was a strong relationship and that something was obviously bothering him.

After a short period, when he did not say anything, she asked, "How does everything go with the alien craft?"

"At the moment, we are just observing its actions, but it is believed that we may have to do battle with it," Blet said in a sombre tone.

"Why must there be a battle?" she asked.

"It was discussed, and all agreed that because of its actions up to this point the craft has been seen to be hostile and that when the time comes, we should be the ones to strike the first blow," Blet replied.

"It is sad that different societies cannot live as one," said Kretyabotkl.

"Yes," said Blet, "that would make things so much easier."

"But for now," he continued, "we must make ready to battle the ones that have already tried to destroy our new world. Then, once we have achieved success, we shall decide on what it is that we are next to do."

"Will it be safe to attack this other craft, knowing that it can cause such damage to something as large as a world?" Kretyabotkl asked.

"Commandling Zaldark and Controller Krerbnot both say that if we remain unseen until we attack, the advantage will be ours and that we should triumph as they will not be expecting it and therefore not be ready," said Blet.

"It is sad," said Kretyabotkl, "that we have come so far to start a new life and that it should begin with a battle."

"Yes, that is unfortunate," replied Blet, "but battles have been fought since time began, and I do not think that they will stop being fought until every living being can learn to respect all others."

"That is indeed a noble sentiment and one that I hope will come true in our lifespan," said Kretyabotkl.

"To think of all the death and destruction that has happened in that time makes me believe that maybe we are not smart enough to live in harmony with others," she added.

"Yes," said Blet, "it does seem strange that we have been able to achieve what we have and yet still cannot find a way to live in peace with others."

"Then I suggest," said Kretyabotkl, "that once we are settled on our new world, it shall be you who will be the overbeing who teaches everyone to live as one with all others."

"A noble sentiment from a true heart," said Blet, "and I am sure, that if there were more like you, it would be possible."

Kretyabotkl looked up at Blet with admiration in her eyes and said, "You are the one to be able to do this, as I can see what it is that you are capable of and how others respect you."

"Unfortunately, not everyone sees me with your eyes," said Blet.

"Then they are blind," replied Kretyabotkl with passion.

Blet shook with what could be said to be the equivalent of laughter.

"I am truly blessed to have one such as you within my core," said Blet, "and hopefully, I will be able to achieve that which you say I should."

"Of this, I have no doubt," replied Kretyabotkl, looking at her sharebeing and wondering why it was, that all others did not see in him what she could see so plainly.

After a few moments, Blet looked around the room and then asked, "Where are the younglings? I have not seen them this past rotation time wise and would like to speak with them."

Kretyabotkl answered, "Etklet said she would take Rlckl to be with a new friend that he has made called Blal, and as for Zcetklot and Bnerkr, they have gone to the training area to watch Commandling Zaldark make sure that the underlings are well trained and able to protect us if the need arises."

"Hopefully they will not be needed, and once this enemy has been destroyed, we shall build a new society that knows the only way we are going to survive will be to live in harmony with others rather than destroy those with which we do not agree," mused Blet.

Kretyabotkl just looked up at her sharebeing and said, "When our younglings, many times over, are living as one with all others, they shall look back with pride and say that they are the descendants of Blet, the overbeing who brought us all together. This is what I believe will happen."

Blet looked at Kretyabotkl with an almost overwhelming sense of admiration, and said, "Well, if that is what you say, then I will have to make it so."

"Please do not make light of what I say," chided Kretyabotkl, "for I can see in your heart that you also know this to be."

"You are right," replied Blet, in a more sombre tone, "but I also know that I will not be able to do this without the support of my core and that you in particular are the one that gives me the strength I need to make it possible for me to be able to achieve these things."

"Then it gladdens me to know that I am able to help you in any way," said Kretyabotkl, holding him just a little tighter.

"You help me in more ways than can be said," replied Blet, looking into the distance and starting to wonder just what may lie ahead.

ANOTHER PLAN 'B'

"OK then," said Raul looking at the others sitting quietly waiting for the meeting to get underway, "would anyone like to start?"

They all looked at each other for a few moments before Julie said, "Yes, I think I may have something that could be of interest."

"Then the floor is yours, Dr Anders," said Raul.

"Thank you, Dr Western," said Julie as the others turned to look in her direction.

"First of all, I think I may have figured out the anomaly."

Watching the reaction of the others, she was a little disappointed with the lack of enthusiasm shown; as she thought that the amount of work that she had put into her findings warranted at least a little recognition.

"Well, that is indeed interesting, Dr Anders," said Raul, "and what was it that you findings revealed?"

"I think it could be a wormhole," she said, and was gladdened a little when she noticed everyone's eyes open just a little wider and they sat up in their seats.

"A wormhole? Are you sure?" asked Dr Peterson.

"As sure as I can be without actually travelling there and seeing for myself," replied Julie.

"I was just about to say that I did not think wormholes existed, until I realized that not that long ago I thought time travel was also impossible," said Gary.

"Yes, well," said Julie, "after all my tests and calculations, it is the only logical explanation."

"That is truly amazing," said Dr Peterson, "to be able to study an actual wormhole. That is going to tell us so much."

"Dr Anders," he continued, "would it be presumptuous of me to ask if I may assist you in your studies of this event?"

"Of course not, Dr Peterson," Julie replied with a smile, "I would be glad of any help."

"Thank you," said Dr Peterson, as he already started to think of some of the tests he might wish to run.

"OK," said Gary, "now obviously I am not an expert on this sort of thing, but could it possibly be a means to us returning to our own time?"

"For what we think we know of wormholes, it would be capable of taking you great distances in space in a relatively short period of time but not through time itself," answered Dr Peterson.

"Also," added Julie, "the fact that it was not there in our time would mean that it could not possibly be our final destination."

"Added to that," Raul then said, "is the fact that this craft was not designed for deep-space travel and would therefore make such a journey not a really viable proposition. I mean, it would not be beyond the realms of possibility, but the amount of time needed to make the journey using thrusters and at the same time trying not to use all of our fuel before we got there—well, let's just say, it would take a very, very long time."

"How long?" asked Gary, "because I'm not doing anything for the next couple of days."

"Well, that would be enough time to get to the Moon," said Raul, looking at Gary sitting back in his seat with a grin on his face.

"Just out of curiosity, how long do you think the journey would take?" asked Tony.

"Without knowing the exact distance or the velocity that we may be able to obtain it would be difficult to say, but you can be certain of one thing and that is that it would take quite a number of years," answered Raul.

"So I take it then, that this isn't going to be plan 'A'," said Gary, still with a grin on his face.

Raul just looked at him and said, "At this stage, I would have to say no."

"Dr Anders," said Dr Peterson, "you said that you had made a 'few' findings, and I was wondering, what else it is that you have found?"

"Yes," said Julie, trying to figure out the best way to word her response.

"As I was studying the anomaly I noticed something else that may impact on us a little more directly."

"And what is that?' asked Raul.

"When we arrived, I was not sure if we got here before the Chicxulub meteor or not. Well, I now think we did, and it's on its way."

"That is indeed interesting," said Raul.

"Sorry," said Gary, not sure that he heard right, "but what is a 'chicken sloop' meteor?"

"The Chicxulub crater is believed to be where the meteor struck that wiped out almost all life on Earth 65 million years ago," explained Julie.

"Oh, I see," said Gary.

"Indeed," said Raul, "and when do you think it will reach us?"

"About two to three weeks is all I can say at this moment," she said, "but obviously I will be able to get a more specific time frame as it gets closer."

"We will be able to dodge it though, won't we?' asked Gary unsurely.

"Well, from what we know about it, it is going to be about 15 kilometres wide, and be travelling at about 60 thousand kilometres an hour, and although it is big and fast, it is not our main concern," said Julie.

"And why would that not be our main concern?" asked Gary, unsure if he was going to like the answer.

"The reason is," she explained, "because we know that it struck the Yucatan Peninsula of Mexico with the aid of a program I have I will be able to plot the continental drift so that I knew where the continents were when it struck, if the Earth is not clouded in dust. But the fact that we know its trajectory as well as its speed means that we should therefore be able to avoid it."

"Then, we have nothing to worry about, right?" said Gary, still not confident in the answer he may receive.

"Not from the meteor, no," said Julie, "but the space rubbish that is travelling with it could be of concern."

Gary looked at Julie quizzically before asking, "Now, by space rubbish, you are not talking of bottles and cans and old car bodies are you?"

"No," replied Julie with a grin on her face, "I mean a debris field around the main meteor, ranging in size from a grain of sand to a city bus, that is spread over an area that could reach a 1000 kilometres."

"Once we know where it is going to hit, couldn't we just alter our course and speed so that we are on the other side of the planet when it does strike?" Gary then asked.

It was Dr Western who answered, "Yes, we would be able to avoid the meteor, but I think the extra dust thrown out from the surface plus the debris field from the meteor would make it extremely dangerous for us to try and navigate our current course."

"OK then, what if we used the impulse gun to just push it away?" was Gary's next question.

"There are a couple of reasons why that may not work," said Raul.

"First of all, the impulse gun is not able to be fired in quick bursts. We could deflect the leading edge of the debris field as well as the meteor itself but trailing particles would still continue on their original courses, and trying to navigate a path through it would not be high on my list of things to do."

"Then," he continued, "is the fact, that there are some that would argue that life on Earth, as we know it to be, could actually have been formed by bacteria that was delivered by a meteor. Who is to say that this is not that meteor, and that, if we were to divert it from impacting the Earth, could we in effect be stopping the formation of life."

He paused before continuing.

"Now, whether this is right or wrong, I for one would not like to take that chance."

"So you're saying that God didn't actually create us and that we are nothing but space germs," said Tony in a rather contemptuous voice.

"No," replied Raul, "I am saying that there are some that think this is how life as we know it, may have been created on Earth."

"Now whether God created the bacteria and sent it to Earth or if it was just a random act of cosmic evolution, I do not know," said Raul, "but what I do know is that I don't want to be the one to prove myself right or wrong by deflecting the meteor."

"Also," he continued, "it still would have had an influence, no matter how miniscule that influence might be, on how Earth evolved."

"That's funny," said Tony, sitting back in his chair with his arms crossed, "because in the Bible, I don't recall seeing anything about dinosaurs or meteors or alien bugs."

"I am not saying that this 'is' what happened Tony, I am saying that this is an alternative view of one part of the scientific community, and I don't believe that we have a right to just say that we don't think this is what happened and therefore whatever we do will be done with impunity. Anything we do that has the possibility to change anything now could have 65 million-year-old ramifications."

"That's pretty old ramifications," said Gary, trying to lighten the mood.

"Yes," said Raul, "a slight change now could have a devastating effect over the course of 65 million years."

"So covering the world in a dust cloud would not be classified as a slight change in the planet's evolution," asked Tony sarcastically.

"If we had arrived after the meteor, I would have had to say yes," replied Raul trying not to rise to Tony's comments, "but the fact that it is on its way, means that now, for the want of a better term, the evolutionary clock will be reset."

Tony did not say anything, and the room started to feel as though it was filling with an uneasy quiet tension.

Finally, it was the quiet was broken when Dr Peterson asked, "So if we cannot divert it and we cannot hide from it and we cannot navigate through the debris field surrounding it, what do you suggest that we do?"

"Well, we may not be able to avoid it whilst in orbit around Earth, but if we do what it is that the craft was designed for, namely head towards the Moon, not only should we avoid the debris field but any rogue particles that escape the meteor's grip would be pulled in by the Moon's gravitational attraction," said Raul.

"As well as the view being absolutely spectacular," added Julie.

"Yes, that it will," said Raul, even though it was not something that really needed confirmation.

Then Tony, realizing that he was not going to be able to sway any body's opinion by arguing with them, asked, albeit still with a slight scowl on his face, "So when do you think we should start our journey?"

"I think if we were to start out at least a week before the meteor gets here that should give us enough time to be able to set up a safe orbit as well as be able to position ourselves so that we have the best possible vantage point," answered Raul.

"So that gives us a week to make sure everything is working as it should and to do a few test fires of the impulse gun,"

"So, Gary, are all the tiles in place?" he then asked.

"Yeah, they're all in, I just need to go over them again to make sure none have shifted since I started," Gary replied.

"This may seem like a silly question," said Dr Peterson, "but are we sure that the tiles are safe to use and that they are not the same as the tiles that exploded in the first place?"

"No, it is not a silly question, Dr Peterson," replied Raul, "but we would have been silly to assume that they were all safe to use."

"We made sure they were all right by checking them with the spectrograph," he then explained.

Next, he asked Tony, "So, are the controls right for us to navigate our way out of orbit?"

Tony, still with a slightly surly look on his face, replied, "It's all working as it should, so it won't be a problem."

"OK, Julie," Raul then said, "if you could keep us updated on the meteors progress, Dr Peterson and I will work on the calculations needed for us to break orbit, and then hopefully, we should have an uneventful journey," he said, looking at each of their faces trying to see how they would all react.

He was gladdened by the fact that he did not see any obvious signs of concern, and apart from Tony's slight pout he sensed an actual positive mood in the room.

After a few seconds, he said, "Well, if no one has anything else to say, we should probably get back to our routines."

As they were getting up and heading off to their respective tasks, Raul went to Tony and said, "Please do not think that I am discounting your beliefs, because I am just trying to deal with the facts that we have at our disposal at the moment and trying to make judgement calls on those facts."

Tony looked at Raul and then said, "I am not someone that has a totally closed mind on the subject, but I do have a great belief in the Bible and I would hope that others could see in it the things that I see. But if this is not the case, then all I can do is pray for them."

"Well, as long as those prayers involve us all being safe, then that would be all I want," said Raul with a smile.

"It would be a shallow person who would pray for anything other than safety for others," replied Tony.

"I do not mean that I think you would not want us all to be safe," said Raul, "I am just saying, that in order for us to make it through this, we all have to look out for each other and realize that we are all part of a team, and that no one individual should be more or less important than another."

"Rhetoric is all good, but I think it is actions that speak louder than words," Tony then said.

"What do you mean?" asked Raul, with a slightly surprised look on his face. "Has someone said or done something to make you feel as though you are not part of this crew?"

"People do not have to necessarily say something for you to know what they actually mean," replied Tony.

"I have to admit that I am a little shocked to hear you say that Tony," said Raul, "and if you tell me what it is that has happened to make you feel this way, I am sure that we can come up with a resolution."

"Yes, I'm sure we can," said Tony sarcastically before turning and saying, "Now, if you will excuse me, I have to go and do some navigation checks."

And with that, he walked off, leaving Raul standing there wondering what had just happened.

As Tony walked away, Gary came up to Raul and asked, "What was all that about?"

"I'm not sure," replied Raul, still with a puzzled look on his face, "but I think Tony's mood swings are letting us know that he might not be handling our situation as well as might be expected."

"So what do you suggest we do?" Gary asked.

"Well," answered Raul, "psychology is not my strong point, so it would only be a guess, but I think at some point soon, we may have to sit him down and talk this through to find out what is going on with him before it gets out of hand and becomes a safety issue."

"Sounds like a plan to me," replied Gary. "And in the meantime, I will keep an eye on him and make sure that he is getting plenty of rest."

"Thanks, that would be good," said Raul.

"So, when will I be able to test fire the impulse gun?" he then asked with a slight change of subject.

Gary thought for a few moments before answering and then said, "I should be able to give all the tiles one more look over on my next walk, so I would think tomorrow we should be right."

"That would be good," said Raul, "and then if all goes well and once we have run a few more diagnostic checks, we should be able to start our journey."

A smile came over Gary's face and he said, "You know, if anyone had asked me when I was walking the beat, where I thought that I might end up, at no time would I have thought to say orbiting the Moon 65 million years ago, and I am pretty sure that if I had, someone may have thrown a large net over me and dragged me away to the funny farm."

"Yes, I don't think too many people would have listed this as a holiday destination," Raul said now with a smile on his face as well.

"But just think if they did, we would have the market cornered," said Gary, trying to look as though he was being serious and not really succeeding.

"OK," said Raul, "but until we get back and you start up your intergalactic, time-travelling space holiday travel agency, I think that you should get ready to check on those tiles."

"OK, Doc," said Gary with a huge grin on his face, "but don't forget, I was going to let you in as a partner."

"Thank you, Gary, but I think one time-travel holiday is all that I would really want," replied Raul.

"Very well," said Gary, "but it will be your loss."

"I'll live with that," said Raul, as he watched Gary turn to go and get suited up for his spacewalk. He turned to head to the control room to run yet more diagnostics, still with the lingering concern of Tony playing on his mind.

JOSHUA GRANGE

As they pulled up in front of the house, Inspector Watts and Deputy Neville saw a large man, who looked as though he could be in his late thirties, standing in the front yard watering the lawn with a hand-held sprinkler attached to a hose.

As they approached, Inspector Watts asked, "Mr Grange?"

"Yes," said the man as he turned towards them.

"I am Inspector Watts and this is Deputy Neville," he said as they both showed their IDs

"We are from IMPol, and we were wondering if you would mind if we asked you some questions?"

"In regards to?" asked Grange with a puzzled look on his face.

"We are actually investigating the Moonshaker incident," answered the inspector.

"Very well," replied Grange, "but I don't see how I will be of any help to you."

"That's all right, sir. We are just following a line of investigation, and your answers may help us tie certain events together," said Inspector Watts.

"OK, I guess it costs nothing to talk," said Grange as he continued to spray water over his lawn and rose bushes, giving the impression of someone that had an attitude that matched his large frame.

"What is your involvement with the AIL?" was the inspector's first question.

"I did not realize that going to church had been outlawed," answered Grange still concentrating on his task at hand.

"If it has, then I would be just as surprised as you," replied Inspector Watts. "I am merely asking what, if any, involvement do you have with the AIL?"

Grange released the trigger on the sprinkler then looked at the two men before answering, "As you obviously already know, yes, I am involved with them, as I go each week to listen to sermons given by Mr Rogerson."

"'Mr' Rogerson, why not Father Rogerson or Pastor Rogerson?" asked Deputy Neville.

"As he is the first to admit he has not served the clergy in a formal way, he is therefore not entitled to be addressed as Father or Pastor or Vicar or Rector or Your Holiness or any other such form, but that still should not be grounds to disallow him the respects of his beliefs," answered Grange with more than a little passion.

"So what do you discuss at these meetings?" asked the inspector.

"Oh, you know, the usual things, like curing cancer, getting rid of poverty, world domination—nothing out of the ordinary," said Grange as he turned back to is task of watering whilst thinking that he hoped that these two would just go away.

"Mr Grange," said the inspector, "the only reason that I am here, is to try and make sense of a seemingly senseless incident. Now, if you do not wish to help in that task, I am sure that there are people in the federal network that would be very interested as to why you would want to hinder this investigation."

Once again, Grange released the trigger on the sprinkler before turning to look first at the inspector, then his deputy, and back to the inspector. He was unwilling to see if the inspector was actually bluffing or not, he then said, "OK, can we just go sit on the porch and I will see if I can help you."

"That would be appreciated," said the inspector.

Once they were all seated, the inspector once again asked Grange, "Now, was there anything in particular that you would discuss at these meetings?"

"Not really," Grange answered, "we would just talk about general things that were currently happening."

"General things such as?" asked Deputy Neville.

"Things ranging from the state of world politics to the moral decline of society and the possible things that could be done to bring about change," Grange replied.

"And what course of action was suggested that you take to bring about these changes?" asked the inspector.

"There were those amongst us who thought that we should be taking a more public approach by holding outdoor rallies, and that way, we could try and connect personally with the people of the streets," replied Grange.

"By people of the streets, do you mean like the homeless and downtrodden and people with minds that could be easily manipulated?" asked Deputy Neville.

"I actually meant the general populace," explained Grange in a slightly superior tone, "so if it were an office worker on a break or a taxi driver waiting for a fare or a homeless person or even an unemployed cowboy, we would not discriminate, and everyone would be able to have their say."

"Did everyone agree with the idea of large rallies?" asked the inspector, knowing full well the answer.

"As I am sure that you have spoken to Graeme Rogerson, it would be foolish of me to say yes, wouldn't it, Inspector?" replied Grange.

"No," he continued, "Graeme Rogerson is a very persuasive speaker, and although there is growing support for more assertive action, he was still able to talk down any action that he thought would bring adverse publicity to the league."

"And how did that make you feel?" asked the inspector.

"How was I supposed to feel, Inspector?" asked Grange, "like a petulant child or a scolded dog, or maybe a person who has been caught trying to sneak out of a restaurant without paying."

"No, Inspector," he continued, "for although I was a little disappointed that the ideas I supported were not adopted, I also know that Graeme Rogerson will not always be in charge and when he is out of the way, the league will be able to move forward the way it should."

"Is the league your only interest, Mr Grange?" asked Deputy Neville. "I mean, do you have a job or are you on any other committees?"

"Yes, I work as a share trader with Notlob, Johnson, and Creer, and, between that and my work with the league, I find I keep myself fairly busy," replied Grange.

"I understand that share trading is a fairly high-stress job," said the inspector, making it seem as though he was taking an interest in Grange's personal life.

"I view it as not so much a job but a career, and as for being high stress, that is just for weaklings who wait for things to happen for them instead of taking control of situations when the need arises," Grange answered with passion.

"So, did you take control of the Moonshaker situation?" asked Deputy Neville.

"No, Deputy," replied Grange, "because I actually agree with Graeme Rogerson, in the fact that I believe that violence is not an answer, merely an outlet, and in the long run, does little to achieve anything."

"Did you hear of anyone else possibly talking about the actions that were taken?" asked Inspector Watts.

"No, Inspector," answered Grange, "and if I had, I can assure you, like Graeme Rogerson, I would have talked them out of it."

"What do you know of Graham Strand?" asked the inspector.

"Only what I see at our meetings at the league, and because of client confidentiality, I cannot discuss my work relationships," replied Grange, which actually took the inspector and Deputy Neville a little by surprise.

"So you were actually trading shares for Mr Strand?" asked the deputy.

"If he wants to trade shares, I am only too interested in helping him, as that is my job," said Grange.

Deputy Neville could not help himself and he said, "I thought you said it was a career."

Grange just looked at him with a blank look on his face before the inspector asked, "Could you tell us what were the main stocks he was trading?"

"I'm sorry, Inspector, but as I have just said, client confidentiality bars me from disclosing that information," Grange replied. "If I were to tell you, I would be barred from trading, and that just ain't gonna happen."

"You are aware that we are actually working very closely with the federal authorities on this, so we are going to be able to find out?" said the inspector, hoping that this might make it seem as though the confidentiality of his client is going to be breached anyway, so he may as well tell and save everyone a little time.

"That's as maybe," said Grange, "but I enjoy my work too much to let you come along and sabotage that. So, if you do have friends in the federal service, then good luck and God speed in finding your information, because I will not give it to you," said Grange definitively.

It was at that moment, the inspector's phone rang.

"Excuse me a moment," he said as he removed it from his pocket and checked the caller ID. "I have to take this," he said and walked to the other end of the porch.

Deputy Neville looked at Grange and then asked, "So how do you become a share trader?"

"It helps if you are able to count past ten," Grange replied with a smirk.

The deputy just looked at Grange with a flat expression and said, "Well, I can count to twenty-five, because that's how many years I can put someone in jail for hindering a federal investigation."

Grange, who was used to being in charge of situations, was momentarily unsure of how to respond.

"Thank you," said Inspector Watts as he closed his phone and placed it back into his jacket pocket.

"Mr Grange, thank you for your time, and if there is anything that you remember, please do not hesitate to call this number," said the inspector, handing him a card.

As Deputy Neville got up and then started following the inspector to the car, he asked, "What's happened?"

"It would appear that Mr Strand received a call from Graeme Rogerson, and then thought it might be a good idea to try and hurriedly leave the country."

"So where is he now?" the deputy then asked.

"He is being held at airport security," replied the inspector. His name was red flagged when he tried to buy a ticket."

"Did they say where he was headed?" was the deputy's next question.

"Sarango," came the reply.

"Interesting choice," said Deputy Neville.

"Indeed it is," said the Inspector, as their car started its speedy journey to the airport.

TIME TO GO

"Controller Krerbnot," said Technician Dseto in a slightly animated voice.

"Yes, Technician Dseto, what is it?" asked Krerbnot.

"The alien craft appears to be altering its course," replied Dseto.

"And what is its new course?" Krerbnot asked.

"I cannot say at this stage," said Dseto, giving him as much information as she could with the facts that she had, "only that it has started to move out of the world's orbit."

"Also," she added, "there were a series of power surges just prior to it altering its course."

"Very well, can you have Overbeing Blet and Commandling Zaldark come to the control room?" said Krerbnot. I think it is time that we discussed in full what we are going to do next.

"Very well, Controller," said Dseto as she activated the personal communicators of Blet and Zaldark.

"Maintainer Zeral," said Krerbnot, as Zeral had just come into the control room to check on some of the monitors covering the ship's operating functions, "Is everything functioning as it should?"

"Everything I can see is doing precisely what it is that it was designed for," replied Zeral, making sure that he checked every detail on the monitors.

"Good," said Krerbnot, as he sat and waited for Zaldark and Blet.

After they had both arrived at the control room and had been told of the alien craft's movements, Zaldark said, "It would appear that they are ready to explore their mineral world."

"How can you be so sure?" asked Blet.

"I would think that they have seen that there will be no resistance from the main world," said Zaldark, "and if they had wanted to leave," he explained further, "they would have done so in the same way that they arrived."

With a curious look on his face, Blet then asked, "But if there is going to be no resistance from the main world, why would they then have to hide themselves?"

Zaldark replied, "It would be, so that if they have enemies, they would be able to travel back and forward without being detected and, therefore, not give away the location of the mineral riches that they have found."

"Then why would they not simply just head straight to the mineral world?" Blet then asked.

Controller Krerbnot answered, "A world of this size will have a grip on any craft circling it. If you wish to break that grip, you have to proceed slowly so that you can ease out of its grip and not try to suddenly jerk yourself free, as this will cause great stress to the craft and not necessarily end in success."

"Would that be why there were power surges detected just before it altered its course?" asked Blet.

"I believe that would be the reason for such a thing," answered Krerbnot.

"Very well, if this is so, then how long before they reach this mineral world?" Blet then asked, not entirely convinced by this logic but not willing to gamble with the lives of all the citizens on board the skyship.

"If this is their destination," answered Krerbnot, "and seeing as how they have only just altered their course, I would think that they could be here in two rotations time wise."

"Commandling Zaldark, will we be ready to defend ourselves if the need arises?" Blet then asked.

"I have been running combat simulations and exercises, and I feel we are ready to win this battle," said Zaldark with pride.

Blet then turned to Krerbnot and asked, "Controller Krerbnot, do you believe we have the capability to win this battle?"

Krerbnot paused for a few seconds before he said, "With Commandling Zaldark's training and the weapons array that this ship has, yes, I believe that we will be victorious."

"Then that is done," said Blet, as he made to turn and leave the room before adding, "and now if you will excuse me, I will seek an audience with the Elders, and let them know of our current situation."

"Very well," said Krerbnot, "I will let you know of any changes to our situation as soon as they happen."

"That will be good," said Blet as he departed, "and may the Great Protector guide us."

LEAVING HOME

"I doubt if I would ever get sick of looking at this sky," said Julie gazing out of the window in awe at the uninterrupted view of space.

"Yes," replied Raul, "without the hindrance of Earth's atmosphere and the reflected light of the sun, things can be seen so much clearer from here."

"And to be able to see the Earth in its entirety, albeit covered in dust, is just amazing," Julie added.

"I am surprised that someone has not actually started a company that takes people on day trips into space," she then said, which caused Raul to splutter into the cup of water that he was drinking at that moment.

Julie turned towards him and asked, "Are you all right?"

"Yes, I'm fine," he said once he had been able to compose himself.

"Did I say something wrong?" she asked with a quizzical look on her face.

"No, it's just that maybe you should speak to Gary about this," he answered.

"Speak to Gary about what?" asked Gary as he entered the room.

"Oh, nothing, it's just that Julie was talking about a space-flight travel agency," explained Raul.

"Really, see I told you it would be a good idea, Doc, and you passed up on the opportunity to get in on the ground floor," said Gary with the ever present smile on his face.

"Silly me," said Raul with mock disappointment. "I don't know what I was thinking."

"Hello, everyone. You sound as though you are all in high spirits."

They turned to see Dr Peterson enter the room.

"Yes, we were just discussing the beauty of our surroundings and how lucky we are to be able to take them all in," said Julie, trying to explain the situation.

"Yes, they are truly amazing," said Dr Peterson.

"You would think," he continued, "that someone with entrepreneurial skills would have thought of some way to cash in on it."

Raul just closed his eyes and dropped his head, whilst Gary, raised his arms with his palms facing upwards and shrugged his shoulders, and Julie, after first looking at Raul and then Gary, just burst into laughter.

Dr Peterson was not really sure of what to think when Raul looked up and said, "Don't worry about it, I think it may be oxygen deprivation."

"Really," said Dr Peterson with a worried look on his face.

"Is it serious, I mean, we are going to be all right, aren't we?" he then asked.

"Yes, it is isolated to just a few," replied Raul.

Gary could see that Dr Peterson was still looking a little bewildered, so he said, "No, truly, Dr Peterson, it is OK."

"If you say so," said Dr Peterson, still not totally convinced, "but I think a problem such as that, would be very serious."

"More than you could imagine," replied Raul.

Then Gary, who was now looking out of the window towards the Moon asked, "Hey, what's that?"

As the others turned to look at Gary and then the direction of his gaze, it was Julie that asked, "What is what?"

"It was something like a reflection," said Gary.

"It could have been a small meteorite that had crashed into the Moon and the sun was just reflecting of any ice it may contain," said Julie, trying to offer an explanation.

"No," replied Gary, "this was just off to the side of the Moon."

"Tony said that he saw something similar a few days ago," said Raul.

"What do you suppose it could be?" asked Dr Peterson.

"Maybe it is an asteroid that had long since disappeared," said Raul, offering up what he thought to be a feasible explanation.

"Goodness me," said Julie, "this trip could be turning into a gold mine of information."

"'Goodness me'," said Gary, "that is an expression that I have not heard since I stayed at my grandmother's house on school holidays."

"I'm sorry," said Julie, "I will try to use something a little more modern next time."

"No," replied Gary, "I am just saying that it is a refreshing change."

"And please," he added, "do not change for the sake of change."

"I did not know that you were so old fashioned," said Julie, who was now the one with a grin on her face. "How chivalrous."

Gary blushed slightly, before stammering, "No, I was just saying, that . . . um . . . I thought that . . . you know . . . I . . . I think it is a nice change."

"It's all right," said Julie with a coy smile, "it is nice to know that chivalry is not dead."

"Yes, well," said Raul, bringing the focus back to their current situation, "we will find out for certain tomorrow, and once we have its coordinates, we will be able to swing by and get a very close look indeed."

"Oh, I can hardly wait," said Julie, feeling like a child the night before Christmas.

"But unfortunately you will have to," said Raul, "and in the meantime, I believe that there are two people who are rostered for rest."

"OK," said Gary, "I was just leaving."

"And I am going as well," said Julie, "although I do not know if I will get much sleep thinking of what we may find tomorrow."

"Yes, well, just remember, that whatever is there will still be there tomorrow, and you need to be rested so that you have a clear head so that you are able to digest any information that we are able to gather," said Raul.

"Of course you are right," said Julie, "but it will still not be easy."

"That's as maybe, but you need to try," was Raul's response.

"Very well then, I will see you in about eight hours," Julie said in a voice of resignation, as she turned and headed towards the sleeping quarters.

"See you then," replied Raul, as he watched her leave.

When she had gone, Dr Peterson turned to Raul and said, "Dr Anders and Gary are becoming good friends, aren't they?"

"Yes," replied Raul, as once again, he found himself checking the computer readouts, "and as long as it does not interfere with their work or compromise our safety, I wish them luck."

"Indeed," said Dr Peterson.

Then unsure of what to say next, just asked, "Is there anything that you would like me to do?"

"Of course," said Raul, going over in his mind, the myriad of things that he would like to check before they got close to the Moon.

SECRETS

"M r Strand," said the inspector as he entered the room and saw Strand sitting at a table with his back to the door, "planning on going on a little holiday were you?"

"I did not realize that I had to have your permission to go on a holiday," said Strand in a slightly smug tone.

"When you are part of an on-going federal investigation," said the inspector, "if you want to go to the bathroom, you need our permission. Also, I think your choice of destinations is more than a little interesting. I mean Sarango. Not a place I would have picked for a holiday destination."

"I was told that it was an inexpensive place to stay, so I thought that I might go for a quick break," said Strand, still maintaining that he did not know that he had done anything wrong.

"So it had nothing to do with the fact that they have no extradition treaty in place with anyone. I mean, how were we going to have one of our chats that we all like so much?" asked Deputy Neville.

"Why do you need to talk to me again anyway?" asked Strand. "I have already told you all I know."

"Have you really?" asked the inspector. "Because we have actually spoken to your stockbroker, and although he did not tell us too much about your dealings with him, we did some checking on the way over here, and it makes quite an interesting story."

Strand, once again made to feel unsure by the inspector, shifted uneasily in his seat.

"I am quite within my rights to buy and sell shares," he said, not really liking where he thought that this conversation was heading.

"You are right, Mr Strand. You are allowed to buy and sell shares," said the inspector, "but the fact that you have a controlling interest in a company called 'Watson Propulsion', which just happens to be the company that lost the bid to use propulsion units to correct the Moon's trajectory to the Moonshaker project, could possibly tell someone that you may have a vested interest in the possible success or failure of that project."

"I told you, I got a phone call and was told what to do," said Strand, feeling more and more isolated the further the conversation went.

"I think it might be time that you dropped the act, because I'm sorry, Mr Strand, but that doesn't really wash any more, and unless you start co-operating, the trouble that you bring down upon yourself will be of epic proportions," said the inspector, looking as though he had finally lost patience with the situation.

After what seemed an eternity but was in reality a few moments, Strand, for the second time since he had met Inspector Watts and Deputy Neville, asked, "What sort of a deal can you offer me?"

Deputy Neville replied, "You tell us everything, and we will make sure that people with names like 'Killer' or 'Crusher' or 'baby-eating, face-slasher Jones', won't be put in the same cell as you."

The inspector looked at his deputy, in what could only be described, as a non-complimentary glance.

"What I think my colleague was trying to say," explained the inspector, "is that you are not really in a position to ask for deals, because no matter what happens from here on in, you are going to jail for a long time."

"But," continued the inspector, "having said that, depending on the information that you are willing to give us, we will be able to tell the prosecuting judge that you were very co-operative."

Strand gave a sigh of resignation and said, "I don't really have much of a choice, do I?"

"More of a chance than the five people who you sent to their death," said Deputy Neville, letting Strand know exactly what he thought of him.

"That was an accident," said Strand, feeling that if he could just clarify his actions, maybe people would understand.

"It wasn't meant to explode," he continued, "it was supposed to just burn out the centre of the dish to show people that it was not dependable."

"What, so then you could come riding in on your big white horse and save the day with your system," said Deputy Neville, with the sound of loathing strong in his voice.

"Like I said, no one was supposed to get hurt," said Strand meekly.

Deputy Neville shook his head and said, "Attaching potentially explosive devices to a craft that is about to go into space wouldn't really be my idea of 'not' trying to hurt anyone."

Strand just looked at the floor and did not reply.

"So, how did you get the tiles there in the first place?" asked the inspector.

"It was Tony Watson," answered Strand.

"The pilot?" asked Deputy Neville.

"Yes," Strand replied.

"What was his involvement in all this?" asked Inspector Watts.

"He was the one that got the tiles onto the base, and then, when everyone was busy looking for more trespassers the night I got in, he and one of the engineers, switched tiles," said Strand, knowing now that the best thing he could do to help himself would be to co-operate fully.

"Obviously, we are going to need the name of the engineer as well as any others that were involved," said the inspector.

"They were the only two," said Strand.

"I hope you are telling the truth, Mr Strand," said the inspector, eyeing Strand warily, "because if you are not and we find out, any deals made will be deemed null and void."

"No, they were the only two," said Strand trying to convince them that he was being truthful. "We thought that it would not be wise to have too many from the league working together on this project."

"So, Rogerson knew about this did he?" asked Deputy Neville.

"Not really," said Strand, "he just knew what I told him."

"And what was that?" the deputy then asked.

"That if all went according to plan, I would be in a position to be able to make a substantial donation for the betterment of the league," said Strand.

"And did he know the details of what it was that you were attempting to do?" asked the inspector, trying to find out if Rogerson was complicit or just naive.

"No," said Strand, "he was more about getting together in meeting rooms and halls and then sometimes getting on hollovision and doing what he did best, talk."

"And you didn't think that this was the right strategy?" asked Inspector Watts.

Strand looked up and said, "There are three types of people in this world, Inspector. Those that make things happen, those that watch things happen, and those that wonder what happened."

"Rogerson," he then said, "was watching and wondering."

"But he was not the one that claimed five lives," said Deputy Neville, not buying into Strand's attempts to justify his actions.

Again, Strand did not answer.

"So how did Tony become involved in all this?" asked the inspector.

"When he started turning up to league meetings, I thought that it might be useful if I started up a rapport with him to see if I could maybe glean some information from him. I did not know that he had a God complex," Strand added.

"What do you mean by 'God complex'?" asked Deputy Neville.

"Apparently," Strand explained, "when he was main test pilot for the air force, he had a few crashes, and the last one was when he was testing the new stealth prototype."

"That's right," said Deputy Neville, remembering hearing about it, "the TR 72."

"Yes," said Strand.

"Some described it as the most horrific crash that they had ever witnessed," he continued, "and being able to walk away from it with only minor injuries gave him a sense of invincibility."

"So he did not think that it was because they were also testing the most advanced personal safety devices that they could fit into the plane?" asked the inspector.

"Obviously not," replied Strand, "and so I was able to play on that and convince him that he had been chosen for this task because he was sure to survive."

"Why would you have said that if no one was supposed to get hurt in the first place?" asked Deputy Neville.

"I knew I had to convince him that this would be a test and therefore only worthy of him," explained Strand.

"And now, he will be able to meet his maker and be told first hand that he is not invincible," said Deputy Neville.

Once more, Strand had nothing to add.

"So, where did you get the tiles from?" asked the inspector.

"There is someone I know who is a master at producing various elements in a basement workshop he has out of town," said Strand.

"So you have a whole network of, for want of a better word, people, helping you destroy anything that stops you from trying to achieve your own personal goals," said Deputy Neville, looking at Strand with an ever-increasing sense of loathing.

"I was about to lose everything," said Strand.

"I was desperate, and I was assured that no one would get hurt," he then said, sounding more and more like a desperate and pitiful person trying to shift the blame, and therefore, not have to take responsibility for his actions.

"Well, if it's any consolation," said Deputy Neville, "you won't lose everything, because you will get free clothing and free food, and you will not have to pay rent, for a very long time."

Strand just slumped forward with his head in his hands, realizing the dramatic change his life had taken.

NEW ENEMIES

"Controller Krerbnot," said Technician Dseto.

"Yes," Krerbnot replied, letting the technician know that he had his attention.

"I now know the course that the alien craft is taking," said Dseto.

"And what is that course?" asked Krerbnot, although feeling as if he already knew the answer.

"It is heading in our direction," came the not totally unexpected reply.

"Very well, have Commandling Zaldark and Overbeing Blet come to the control room immediately," said Krerbnot in a tone that let Dseto know that immediately, meant immediately.

"Very well, Controller," said Dseto without question.

After they had both arrived and Krerbnot had briefed them on what was taking place, Blet asked the first question.

"Do you think that they know we are here?"

"I do not think so," Krerbnot answered.

"And what do you base those thoughts on?" Blet then asked.

"It is the leisurely pace at which they are travelling," explained Krerbnot.

"If they thought that there was a chance of attack, they would be making a more erratic and swift approach."

"I would have to agree," said Zaldark. "You do not move slowly into battle and afford your enemy an easy target. Also, seeing what they have done to the main world, I think they would have already attacked us if they knew we were here."

"So what do you propose that we do?" asked Blet.

"Although they have not yet seen us, I will move us closer to the mineral world so that we will be even harder to spot," said Krerbnot. "Then, when they are close enough, we shall surprise them with our own attack."

"And are we certain of victory?" asked Blet.

"In matters of war, Overbeing, victory is never assured until after the battle," said Zaldark.

"But one thing is always certain," he continued, "and that is, surprise is often better than any weapon."

After a few moments, Blet said, "Very well, if this is what must be done, then this is what must be done."

Krerbnot turned to Technician Zetkr and said, "Take us on a course so that we may be closer to the mineral world."

"As you say, Controller," Zetkr replied, as the ship started to slowly turn towards the Moon.

Then, speaking to Commandling Zaldark, Krerbnot next said, "Commandling, make sure that the troops and weapons are ready for battle."

"They are ready for both battle and victory," was Zaldark's reply.

"Then let it begin," said Krerbnot, knowing that he had to show no outward sign of trepidation.

OLD ACQUAINTANCES

"Are you ready to make some new, very old discoveries?" asked Raul.

"This is so exciting," said Julie, "I am—"

"Oh, my great green gravy," said Gary, interrupting Julie mid-sentence and then pointing out the window. "What is that?"

As they looked to see what it was that had gotten Gary's attention, they could just make out in the distance the sun glistening on what appeared to be a great silver craft, moving slowly towards the Moon.

Nobody was able to say anything as they were all dumbstruck at seeing a craft, obviously from another planet.

Gary was first able to speak, and he could only manage, "Is that a—?"

"It's a space craft," said Dr Peterson.

"It would appear so, yes," Raul then said.

"OK, so what do we do now?" asked Gary.

"I'm not sure," replied Raul.

"Do you think that they have seen us?" Julie then asked.

"Again, I am not sure," answered Raul, "but by the way they appear to be moving towards the Moon, may indicate that they do not want to initiate contact and that they could actually be trying to hide in the shadows."

"Why would they want to do that?" asked Dr Peterson. "I mean, it is not like we are going to attack them."

"Well, obviously, they know as much about us as we know about them, so maybe they want to study us before they decide what it is that they want to do," Raul answered.

"What do you mean, before they decide what to do?" asked Dr Peterson.

"I would say that they will want to see if we pose a threat or not," explained Raul.

"But why would they think that we want to threaten them?" was Dr Peterson's next question.

"I think this is what my father meant when he told me that if you treat every stray dog as a friend, one day you will get bitten," said Gary, hoping that this would help Dr Peterson understand.

"Well, what can we do to show them that we mean them no harm?" asked Dr Peterson, starting to become a little more alarmed.

"I think if we can remain calm," said Gary, "that might help."

Dr Peterson did not say anything, but he still did not feel totally relaxed.

"What about it, Doc? Could we get them on the radio?" Gary then asked, as his police training that taught him to remain calm and think through a crisis started to take control.

"We could give it a try," said Raul, not sounding absolutely convinced that it would work.

"But," he continued," for us to find the same frequency and bandwidth, would be like trying to find a diamond in the desert."

"Not great odds, but still worth a try," Gary replied.

"Yes, you're right. I mean it won't hurt to try will it?" answered Raul.

Unsure of what to say as he leaned towards the microphone, Raul finally settled on, "Unidentified craft, this is Dr Raul Western of the Moonshaker project. Can you hear us?"

"Please respond," he added as an afterthought.

No one spoke, and after a silence of about ten seconds, he tried again.

"Unidentified craft, this is the Moonshaker satellite from Earth, can you hear us?"

THE FIRST PUNCH

"Controller Krerbnot," came a comment in a highly animated voice.

"What is it, Technician Dseto?" asked Krerbnot.

"All of our systems are somehow being attacked," answered Dseto.

"What do you mean, attacked?" asked Krerbnot unsure of what to think.

"There is an interference causing all of our systems to shut down," said Dseto doing her best to explain.

"What is this interference?" Krerbnot then asked.

"It seems to be coming from the alien craft," Dseto said.

This was not news that Krerbnot was expecting, or wanted.

Zaldark then said, "Obviously, they have spotted us but were not ready for an assault and are using some kind of disruption weapon to gain enough time before they mount a full attack."

Krerbnot turned to Zaldark and said, "We must attack at once, as the element of surprise is no longer ours."

"I agree," said Zaldark, who then turned to one of his underlings who had been positioned at the weapons console and gave the order to start the attack.

After a few seconds of inactivity, the underling turned to Zaldark with news he was not sure that he wanted to give.

"Commandling," he said.

"What is it? Why are we not attacking?" asked Zaldark in a sharp tone.

"Our weapons systems are not functioning as they should," replied the underling.

"Can we attack or not?" asked Zaldark impatiently.

"We will be able to launch an attack from the weapons room, but our guidance system cannot be used," answered the underling, desperately trying to contact his colleagues in the weapons room.

"I may not have a military mind," said Blet, "but I would think that if you cannot aim you weapons, you will have little chance of hitting your target."

"That is true, Overbeing," said Zaldark, "but if we launch multiple weapons at one time, not only will it greatly increase our chances of destroying our enemy, but the fact that there are multiple weapons being fired means that they have more to concentrate on and greatly reduces their ability to mount an effective counterattack.

"And to increase our chances even further," he added, "we must close the gap between us whilst they think they have us immobilized and before they can attack, because I think if they had been able to, they would have already destroyed us."

"First weapons away," said the underling, watching his monitor that was still able to at least track the weapons fired.

"Navigator Shetklot," said Krerbnot, turning to his main navigator, "are we still able to move closer to the alien craft?"

"It can be done, but I will have to use the controls on the direct system," his navigator answered.

It was called the direct system, although in reality it was far from direct, because it was linked to the thrust and navigation controls by a series of linkages and cables allowing for rudimentary control of the skyship in just such a circumstance.

After he had gone to the front of the control room and removed the cover panel of the direct control console, revealing three short levers and a series of gauges, he then swung around and locked the seat that fitted into the console, sat, and after a few seconds said, "I now have control of the skyship, Controller."

"Very good," said Krerbnot, "now take us towards our enemy at attack speed."

"It will be done, Controller," came the reply.

"Next weapons away," said the underling, knowing that the closer they got, the greater the chance of hitting the target.

FITTING FINALE

*N*ews broadcast:

"In a breaking story, several members from the AIL, have been questioned by police today in regard to the "Moonshaker incident,'" said the news reader.

"Although nothing has been confirmed, it is believed charges could be laid as early as tomorrow in direct response to the tragedy. More news as it comes to hand.

"And in a related story, Watson Propulsion, the company that lost the Moon correction bid to the Moonshaker project, has had its trading rights frozen until the investigation into the AIL has been completed.

"The weather for the next couple of days should be cloud free and a lovely twenty-four degrees, so we should have a glorious day for the memorial service to those five brave souls that gave their lives trying to save our planet."

"Why are you watching that?" asked Stephanie. "You know it is only going to upset you."

"I cannot understand how someone could do something like that," replied Tania.

"I mean, Raul was trying to help everyone, and for this to happen, it's just . . ." she said without actually finishing the sentence.

"Well," said Stephanie, "as that inspector said, it seemed to have been driven by greed and that can be a powerful motivator."

"But to place money over life, what sort of a monster does that?" Tania then asked, knowing it to be a rhetorical question.

Stephanie just looked at her sister and shrugged her shoulders, knowing that no answer could properly explain the actions of some people.

After a short period of silence, Stephanie finally thought it was time to bring up the subject that she had been pondering since the tragedy.

"Tania," she said, "Murray and I were thinking, that if you wanted to, there would be no reason for you to stay here on your own and that you could come home with me, as we have plenty of room and you know that you would be more than welcome—as well as the fact that you would not just be sitting here worrying yourself sick over what has happened."

Tania looked at her sister and was unsure of what she felt.

When she was able to gather her thoughts, she said a little angrily, "This house belongs to Raul and me, and whilst Ellie is still out there somewhere, I would not dream of abandoning it."

"I am not saying that you should leave it for good," said Stephanie trying to explain. "I just mean that maybe you could stay for a while, because I really do not want to leave you on your own."

"And," she continued, "Whether you stay for a few weeks or a few months, it does not matter, only that you know we are there for you."

Tania thought before next speaking and then said, "I need to be here when they find Ellie."

"The authorities are doing all they can," said Stephanie, "and if they find her, they will know what to do, and obviously, you will be the first one they contact. You could be back here in a matter of hours."

"It is not a matter of 'if' they find her," Tania said, getting a little angry with her sister again, "but 'when' they find her, and when they do, I do not want to be hours away, I want to be right here where she needs me."

"I do wish that you would consider it, Tan," Stephanie said, "because I can only stay for a few days after the service. Then I have to go back to work, and I can't expect Murray to do everything around the house as well as his job."

"Stephanie, I have already said that I will be fine," replied Tania, "and if you have to go back, that is quite all right.

"And," she continued, "if I have to stay here on my own for the rest of my life, then that will be OK as well."

"Oh, that is just not going to happen, young lady," said Stephanie, mimicking something that their mother used to say when either of them would argue with her.

Tania looked up at her sister with a smile spreading across her face and said, "It used to be so final when she would say that."

"Yes," said Stephanie, "but unfortunately, she is not here now and it is up to us to look out for each other."

Tania sighed and then said in a voice of slight resignation, "OK, I will think about it and we will talk after the service."

"I think you would be making the right choice," said Stephanie.

"I did not say I would go," Tania replied, "merely that we would talk about it."

Stephanie looked at her sister and said with maybe a little too much enthusiasm, "That's fine, but just think, if you did come back with me, if you wanted, you could rent or even sell this place and make a fresh start and maybe even go back and finish your studies."

"Stephanie," replied Tania reproachfully, "I said that I only wanted to talk it over, not that I had agreed to anything. So please, do not start mapping my life out as though I have no say in it."

"You're right," said Stephanie, feeling as though she would be able to talk her sister around to her ideas. "I am getting a little ahead of myself."

"We will talk after the ceremony," she said, realizing, that maybe she should not push her sister so hard. "Now, what are we going to have for lunch, because I am more than a little peckish?"

"I am not really that hungry," replied Tania.

"Well this time little missy, you are going to listen to me, because you have to eat and I am not going to stand by and let you make yourself sick," said Stephanie in her father's best scolding tone.

"Yes, Dad," said Tania with the smile returning to her face as she got up and joined her sister as they both then walked to the kitchen.

BACKHAND RETURN

"Unidentified craft, this is Dr Raul Western of the Moonshaker project. Are you receiving?"

"Oh, they are starting to move," said Julie, as they then all looked and saw the strange craft move away from the Moon and start to head in their direction.

"What's that?" asked Dr Peterson, as he noticed what appeared to be sparkling orbs being discharged from the alien craft.

"I am not sure," replied Raul, "but I do not think—" is all he could say before the first orb exploded harmlessly away from the craft.

Next, the second and third orb exploded, each time getting closer and closer but still far enough away so as to cause no damage.

"What's going on?" asked Tony as he came running into the control room.

"We would appear to have friends, who are not very friendly, trying to knock on our door," said Gary pointing out the alien craft in the ever diminishing distance.

Tony looked in slack jawed astonishment at the approaching craft.

"What are we going to do?" asked Dr Peterson, in a slightly excited voice as he noticed three more orbs being dispatched from the alien craft.

"Well, for starters, I don't think we should panic," said Gary. "But we obviously can't outrun them, and if we stay here long enough, we are going to be destroyed," he added as the three orbs exploded, still far enough away so as not to cause any damage but close enough to rock the Moonshaker.

"So that leaves only one option, and that is to fight."

"I'm sorry," said Tony sarcastically, "but I seemed to have left my bazooka at home.

"How are we supposed to fight without any weapons?" Tony then asked, all the while becoming more and more agitated.

"A weapon can be anything you have at your disposal used in the right way," said Gary, as Julie then said, "Three more of those sparkly things are coming."

"Doc," said Gary in an authoritative voice, "can you arc up the impulse gun, and Tony and I will turn this thing around so that we can fire it at the alien craft."

"Will that work?" asked Dr Peterson.

"We will soon find out," replied Gary, as they all saw the first orb explode well before it reached them.

As the Moonshaker started to turn, everyone inside watched, as the second orb exploded so closely that it rocked the Moonshaker violently, and the third one, was on what appeared to be a collision course.

Everyone held their breath, as they watched it get closer and closer, until it eventually reached and then passed them without incident, continuing its path into the blackness of space.

Gary, hands shaking slightly from the adrenalin being created by his body due to the fact that he had just thought he had drawn his last breath, got the Moonshaker pointed in the direction needed to be able to be fired at the alien craft.

"Doc, how soon before we can fire?" asked Gary, as he saw yet another three orbs heading their way, and because the alien ship was now starting to loom large in their view, he knew that time was running short.

"It is at 10, 12, 15, 18 per cent," said Raul, reading off the power increments as they showed.

"OK, just be ready to fire as soon as I say," said Gary, knowing that they may only get one shot.

"25, 29, 35," said Raul, as Gary watched both the orbs, and the alien craft, get ever so much closer.

"41, 47," said Raul, hand poised to fire, and making sure he remembered to hit 'fire' and then 'yes', as Gary watched the orbs get as close as he thought would be safe, and then said loudly, "Now."

Raul immediately pressed the fire button, and almost before the computer could ask if he was sure he wanted to fire, he had pressed 'yes'.

The Moonshaker vibrated slightly as the impulse gun fired with a low "whumph" and a shock wave was sent towards the alien craft.

The next thing they all saw was that the sparkling orb closest to them was immediately stopped and then thrown back towards the alien ship, as were the other two.

Then, the alien craft was thrown violently into a rearward trajectory when the shock wave and sparkling orbs reached it.

Gary did not know if the shockwave alone would have caused much damage, but the explosions caused by the orbs that struck the craft as they had been thrown back, was bound to have done something to the structure.

Of this he was certain.

"Is that it?" asked Julie, as she, with the others, watched as the alien craft, went tumbling rapidly out of view.

"I'm not sure," said Gary, "but if we have not stopped it, we certainly gave it a bloody nose, and hopefully, that will be enough so that they won't want to come back."

"But where would it have come from?" asked Julie. "I mean, there are no other inhabitable planets within light years of this area."

"Yes, well," said Raul, "if I had to hazard a guess, which is all any of us can do at this stage, because of its size, I do not think it was designed for short trips.

"As well as the fact," he added, "that we have no way of knowing how fast it can travel or how long it has been travelling."

Dr Peterson then asked, "Could it have come through the wormhole?"

"That is an interesting question, Dr Peterson," said Raul.

"Julie, would it be possible for a craft of that size to make such a journey?" he then asked.

"If the wormhole was stable enough and the craft of solid construction, I do not see why not," replied Julie. "And from my preliminary observations, I would say that the wormhole would be both solid enough and large enough to allow that vessel to pass."

"And the fact that it did not disintegrate when it was hit by those exploding things would tell us that it was solid enough," said Gary, "but I think the question we must ask, is whether it will be coming back or not, and if it does, what are we going to do?"

The question actually brought the sober realization of their situation back to them all.

"Could we not just use the impulse gun again?" asked Dr Peterson.

"It worked once because they obviously were not expecting it," replied Raul, "but the chance of them not being ready for it the second time, I think would be very slim."

"But having said that," he continued, "I think as it is our only means of defence, we are going to have to try, but this time, we will have to be ready, and at 100 per cent so that, if we can hit them, they will not be able to recover."

"So, you're saying that they would have the same level of intelligence as us," said Tony in a hostile voice.

Raul was taken slightly aback by Tony's outburst, but was still able to compose himself enough to answer.

"The fact that they are able to create and then navigate such a craft, would, I think, place them in the very intelligent category."

"What," said Tony with more than a little venom in his voice, "you're saying that these godless creatures are our equals?"

"Whether they are godless or not, has got nothing to do with this," said Raul, "but what does is that we may possibly have to battle a foe that is bent on destroying us."

Tony stared at Raul then the others, and said, "Maybe you should all just have some faith," before turning and leaving the room.

After a few seconds Gary said, "It's bad enough we've got some extraterrestrials trying to blow us up, now we have to start worrying about Tony losing the plot."

"No, it is not what I would call an ideal situation," said Raul.

"So what are we going to do?" asked Julie.

"At this stage, I think all we can do, is try and keep an eye on him and hopefully calm him down," answered Raul. "But what I think we should do first, is check to see if we sustained any damage in the attack."

"OK," said Gary, "I'll get suited up and check on the dish."

"Good," said Raul, "and Julie, I think you should see if you can locate that ship and watch its movements."

"I'll try," said Julie, knowing her task would not be a simple one, as she knew that in space you would only have to be off your target area by a fraction of a degree and you could be looking at something that is millions of kilometres away from what it is that you are trying to find.

"And Dr Peterson," Raul then said, "I will get you to help me run yet more diagnostics, to ensure that all our systems are still working as they should."

"Very well," replied Dr Peterson, feeling glad to be a part of the team.

"OK, let's go," said Raul, trying to sound upbeat, but feeling more than a little concerned about the situation with Tony, as well as wondering what they would do if the alien craft did in fact return.

A MATTER OF HONOUR

"Weapons on target," said the underling at the weapons console.

They all watched in anticipation for the expected explosion that would destroy their foe.

The next statement from the underling dashed those hopes momentarily, when he said, "Second weapon misfired early. Third weapon malfunction; no damage to report."

"Keep firing," said Zaldark, knowing that as the distance closed it would only be a matter of time before the alien craft was destroyed.

"Controller," said Technician Dseto, "the craft is turning away."

"It would appear," said Krerbnot, "that they would rather flee than do battle."

"They must not be allowed to escape," said Zaldark in a voice full of urgency, "because if they do, they will be free to return with a force that would be large enough and prepared enough to reclaim their prize."

"Weapons away," said the underling.

Everyone watched, as the weapons got closer and closer to their target, until they were halted and then thrown back towards the skyship at great speed.

"Detonate! Detonate!" yelled Zaldark at the underling, knowing that if the weapons were to impact on the skyship it might not survive.

The underling acted immediately and was relieved to see the weapons explode before reaching the skyship, but before he could report, he, like everyone else on board, was thrown violently towards the front of the ship, as the shockwave from the impulse gun suddenly reversed the skyship's direction of travel.

The five seconds or so that it took Krerbnot to regain his senses, after crashing first over the consoles in front of him and then into the forward area of the ship, along with the others, meant that the ship had tumbled uncontrollably for many of reels.

Fortunately, the Krandon Crystals seemed to be functioning as they should, and although the sky seemed to be rotating and spinning in all directions, everyone still had firm footing, and the only problem from watching those near, large viewing windows would be a sense of extreme vertigo.

"Navigator Shetklot!" Krerbnot called out, looking at the bodies strewn all over the floor.

"Controller," said Shetklot slowly picking himself up.

"Can you regain control of the ship?" Krerbnot asked him.

"I shall try," said Shetklot as he winced in pain when he lifted his left arm.

"Are you well?" asked Krerbnot seeing Shetklot's obvious discomfort.

"I am able to perform my task," replied Shetklot as he sat back at his station and tried to regain control of the skyship.

"Is everyone else able to perform their tasks?" Krerbnot next asked, as he knew that the first thing to do was to gain control of the situation before tending to the injured.

After a few seconds, Technician Zetkr attracted attention to himself by calling out with urgency in his voice, "Controller Krerbnot, over here."

As Krerbnot walked to Zetkr he noticed the two bodies lying close to each other.

The first thing he noticed was the odd angle of the legs and the head in relation to the torso.

He immediately knew that Commandling Zaldark, would not be issuing any more orders.

As for the second body, that of Overbeing Blet, he could see what appeared to be a dent in his side, where maybe he had been thrown against the corner of a console, and Krerbnot was sure that his injuries were not going to be minor.

"Technician Dseto," Krerbnot called out.

"Yes, Controller," came the reply.

"Get Healer Retkrotz here straight away," said Krerbnot, making sure his command was definite, because he knew that time could not be wasted by someone not understanding what it was that he wanted.

"Of course, Controller," said Dseto, hoping that the communicator would still work.

It did.

"Overbeing Blet," said Krerbnot as he leaned over the prone figure lying on the floor, "can you hear me?"

After a few seconds of no response, Krerbnot gently touched Blet's shoulder and asked again, "Overbeing Blet, can you hear me? Are you all right?"

Blet opened his eyes with a groan and said, "I hear you, Controller. What is happening, what of our enemy?" he then asked as he tried to get up.

The searing pain that he immediately felt in his side caused him to collapse back onto the floor.

"You should not move," said Krerbnot, "Healer Retkrotz will be here soon, and he will start your path to recovery."

"I feel it may be a long path without an ending," said Blet, knowing within himself, that his injuries were not minor.

"That will be for Healer Retkrotz to say," said Krerbnot, not allowing himself to harbour any negative thoughts.

"What of the alien craft?" Blet then asked with a labouring breath.

"You should not try to speak," said Krerbnot, knowing that it was already starting to become more difficult for him to even stay awake.

"But here is Healer Retkrotz. He will soon have you on your feet," said Krerbnot, not liking to see someone, who he thought of not so much as an authority figure but maybe someone that he could one day call a friend, lying helpless on the floor.

Knowing that sentimentality was something that he could not afford at this point, he turned to his navigator and asked, "Have you control of the ship, Navigator Shetklot?"

"It is steering straight but slow," was Shetklot's reply.

"Very well. Technician Zetkr, do we know where the alien craft is?" he then asked.

"It would appear that it did not follow us, as I cannot find it on our scanners," answered Zetkr, as he had returned to his work console.

"Starguide Zyaot," Krerbnot said as he turned and saw her at her console, "where are we in relation to the new world?"

When she turned to answer, Krerbnot saw the blood flowing freely out of the right side of her head.

As she tried to answer, all she could do was mumble something incoherently, before she too collapsed onto the floor.

Krerbnot rushed to aid his stricken starguide.

As he got to her, he immediately took off his outermost garment so that he might use it to stem the flow of blood.

Whilst he was holding the makeshift bandage to her head, and at the same time asking anyone for something to use as a pillow so that she may be made more comfortable, Zyaot looked at Krerbnot and said, "Forgive me, Controller, I have failed you."

"You have failed no one, Starguide Zyaot, you have done you job with both bravery and honour and when you have recovered . . ." is all he could say before he realized that she was now with the Great Protector.

At that moment, Krerbnot looked at the chaos surrounding him, and silently vowed, that the alien craft would pay for what it had done.

In the hours after the attack, when Blet had been taken back to his quarters and Zaldark and Zyaot had been placed with the other casualties from all over the ship in the designated areas until such a time would permit that a proper ceremony could be held, Krerbnot busied himself with making sure that damages and injuries were treated as best as possible.

After he had made sure that this was happening, he headed to a meeting with his key personnel, amongst whom were his new starguide, Stbetsho, and the new commandling, Ciotglerz.

At least he was thankful that the sayers were not harmed.

When he arrived at the meeting hall, he was glad to see that almost everyone was there, and so he decided that they should start straight away.

"Thank you all for coming," said Krerbnot getting the meeting underway.

"I would like to congratulate Commandling Ciotglerz on his appointment, as well as Stbetsho on becoming a starguide."

"Also, I would like to welcome Zcetklot, who, as Overbeing Blet's eldest youngling, will be taking his place until such a time that Overbeing Blet can return."

"Now, Maintainer Zeral, how are the repairs to our ship progressing?" was his first question.

"They will be completed in less than one rotation time wise," Zeral replied.

Next he asked Technician Dseto, "Do we have full control of the skyship's systems?"

"We have checked all of our systems and are currently repairing those at fault," explained Dseto. "I believe that we will have full control in less than one half of one rotation time wise."

The door to the meeting hall opened, and Healer Retkrotz entered.

"I am sorry for my tardiness," he said as he took his seat.

"Healer Retkrotz, there is no need for you to excuse yourself," said Krerbnot.

"Our circumstances tell us that we may not always be able to keep to an exact timetable," he then said, trying to alleviate any anxiety that Retkrotz may be feeling.

"Thank you for your words, Controller," Retkrotz replied.

"So, can you tell us of the injuries to our citizens?" Krerbnot then asked.

Retkrotz sighed before answering, and then said, "There are twenty-five citizens that have gone to the Great Protector, and there are seventy-three more with injuries that will require further attention."

Krerbnot, although saddened by the loss of so many citizens, knew that the grieving process would have to wait, and so he then asked Ciotglerz, "Commandling, how is it that our weapons had no effect on the alien vessel?"

"It would appear, Controller, that they have a weapon that we have not come across before," said Ciotglerz, trying his best to explain what it was that he thought he knew, "and that somehow, it was able to take control of our weapons and turn them against us.'

"How is this possible?" Krerbnot asked, knowing that the best way to defeat something is to know how it works.

Maintainer Zeral answered, "We believe that it may have something to do with the interference that was used by the alien craft to disrupt our control systems."

"How can this be?" Krerbnot then asked.

"It would appear that there was a hidden signal sent with the interference that was able to take control of our systems and therefore, make our weapons, their weapons," said Zeral. "Also, it would appear that the signal was somehow able to react with the blast of the weapons, and that is what we believe caused us to travel such a vast distance from the battle."

Krerbnot thought for a few moments before asking, "Will it be possible to block this signal?"

Technician Dseto answered, "Given enough time, I believe we would be able to figure out exactly what the signal is and therefore be able to block it completely."

"Unfortunately, I don't think time is something that we have a great deal of," said Krerbnot.

"Because," he explained, "now that they know of our presence, I am sure the alien craft, will seek reinforcements."

"There may be another way," said Zeral.

"And what is that?" asked Krerbnot in hopeful anticipation.

"The alien craft may be able to take control of the skyship's systems, but what if we were to use a weapon that was independent of those systems?" said Zeral.

"But all of our weapons are controlled by the skyship's systems," said Ciotglerz.

"That is true," replied Zeral, "but when is a weapon not a weapon?"

When no one answered, he then said, "When it is not a weapon at all."

"I do not understand," said Krerbnot.

"The one thing that can be used independently from all of the skyships systems is the Terra Shaper," said Zeral.

"But that is just to shape the surface of our new world," said Ciotglerz, thinking that Zeral had no idea of battle.

"That is true, Commandling Ciotglerz, but if it can reshape a world, I do not think that it would have much difficulty in piercing a small space vessel," Zeral replied.

"Can this be done?" asked Krerbnot becoming enthusiastic about the idea.

"There is an area directly below the control room where it could be set up," said Zeral outlining his idea.

"Once there, it would be in direct line with the skyship, so that whatever direction we were facing, would be the line of the Razon beam," explained Zeral.

"And," he continued, "it could be controlled by no more than two personnel, one being an underling, and the other, a maintainer who has experience with the Terra Shaper."

"Will it be safe to travel with the area open so that they may be able to fire the beam?" asked Krerbnot.

"Yes," replied Zeral.

"Once they have their personal atmosphere devices on, we can isolate the forward portion of the area, so that we do not lose too much of our own atmosphere," said Zeral reassuringly.

"What distance from the alien craft would we need to be before it would have an effect?" Krerbnot then asked.

"Because the Razon beam is narrow, we would have to be close enough so as to have a greater chance of hitting our target, but the beam itself would be lethal for many spans," replied Zeral.

"How long before this can be done?" asked Krerbnot.

"With my maintainers and Commandling Ciotglerz's underlings, it could be done in no more than two long time periods," answered Zeral.

"Then that is what must be done," said Krerbnot, before adding, "and may the Great Protector have pity on our enemies."

WHAT MUST BE DONE

"General Fredrickson, thank you for coming."

The statement was made by Councillor Leparge.

"Of course, Councillor, I am always at your call," replied the general, feeling that with current events unfolding, he was about to be given some good news.

"As you are no doubt well aware," said the councillor, "the main opposition to your project has, for want of a better term, been shut down. Now this means, obviously, that the Moonshaker program will need to be up and running again as soon as possible, because there is something that our scientists have found that no one has been told about yet."

The general had a quizzical look on his face when he asked, "And what would that be, if I am allowed to ask?"

"Of course, General," replied the councillor.

"It is the fact that they have found the rate of the Moon's descent is increasing, and if we do not act swiftly to correct it, it may be as early as twenty years when the effects could create devastating consequences on Earth."

"Very well then," the general said, taking in and analysing the information just given to him, "as we cannot afford to waste time, I will assemble the key personnel immediately and give them their instructions."

"We shall arrange a press conference for you tomorrow morning, once you have assembled your team," said Councillor Weddell.

"We will be ready," said the general, knowing full well that if he had to he would handpick every person for this next build and that the security checks that were going to be carried out would tell him absolutely everything there was to tell about any detail on any person entering the building site. He also knew, that if they failed this time, they may not get another chance.

WAITING

"Any sign of our friends yet?" asked Raul.

"I haven't been able to locate them so far," replied Julie, "but it is very difficult to be able to locate the exact same spot in space, every time we come around."

"Yes, well, just do your best," said Raul, not really knowing what to say in a situation such as the one they currently found themselves in.

Julie looked at him and asked, "Are you OK?"

After a few seconds, Raul turned and said, "I was going to be big and brave and say 'yes, of course' and just brush away anybody's concerns, but the truth is, I am concerned with our current situation, and I sometimes wonder, could I have done anything differently to avoid what happened."

Julie replied as reassuringly as she could, "I think that the fact that we are here now actually creates unique opportunities that we should take advantage of, and when the time comes, I also think, that the people needed to rectify our circumstances are here right now as well."

"And," she added, "unless your middle name is Nostradamus, I think it would have been very difficult to have known what was going to happen."

Raul smiled and then said, "I thought I was the one that was supposed to give pep talks."

"Everybody could do with a little reassurance every now and then, just to let them know that they are appreciated," said Julie.

"And as I just said, I think if anyone can get us back, it is you, Dr Peterson, and Gary."

"What's this, mentioning my name with me not being here to defend myself? Slanderous," said Gary as he entered the control room.

Raul looked in his direction and said, "Julie was just singing your praises in being able to deliver us from all manner of predicament."

"Really," said Gary, "so that is something else I will have to add to my résumé, 'Predicament Deliverer'."

Raul chuckled and then said, "Suddenly I feel so much better."

"Ah, another successful mission," said Gary with his ever-present smile.

"Now," he then said in a slightly more sombre tone, "how are we situated with our unhappy neighbours?"

"I have not been able to locate them yet," replied Julie, "but if they do return, the closer they get, the better the chance I will have of spotting them."

"The problem will then be what to do when they return," said Dr Peterson, entering the control room.

"Oh, Dr Peterson," said Julie with a slight jump, "you gave me such a start."

"I am sorry, Dr Anders, it is just that you were so engrossed in your conversation, I did not want to interrupt you," explained Dr Peterson.

"It's fine," said Julie, feeling slightly embarrassed. "I am sure that I will survive."

"Very well," said Dr Peterson, before once again asking, "so what are we going to do if they return?"

"That is a good question, Dr Peterson," said Raul, thinking of a response.

"Please," said Dr Peterson, "if everyone else is being informal, I think it might be time that you called me by my first name, Ashley."

"Very well then, Ashley," answered Raul, "I think our options are somewhat limited."

"The fact that we were able to hit them with the impulse gun means that we now know that we have a capable weapon."

"But whether they will give us a chance to use it again, may remain to be seen."

"And," he continued, "we know that we cannot outrun them, so if they do return, it could get very interesting."

Ashley then asked, "What if we did not have to outrun them?"

Raul looked at him with a puzzled expression on his face and asked, "What do you mean?"

"Well, you know how we did not see our visitors until we started heading straight for them? What if we were the ones hiding. I mean, we are nowhere near as big as they are, and if they can't find us, maybe they will think that we were destroyed and just leave," said Ashley, in hope more than anything.

"The problem with that Dr Pe . . ., sorry, Ashley, is that there are not too many places to hide," said Gary.

"Not here, no, but what if we were on the dark side of the Moon?" Ashley explained. "We would be able to move in closer and hide in the shadows, and eventually, they would get tired of searching for us and leave."

"That could be a good idea, if we were not restricted by our own vessel," said Raul.

"What do you mean?" asked Ashley.

"If we were to stop circling the Moon and at the same time get closer, we would crash down to the surface, and although it only has one fifth of the gravitational pull of Earth, if we did survive, I am fairly sure we would not have enough power to lift off again.

"And," he continued, "the fact that we would run out of power as the solar cells would have nothing with which to recharge our batteries means that we would perish rather quickly."

Nobody spoke, as Raul's last statement made every one realize the severity of their current situation.

"Anyway," said Raul, "who is to say that they are going to return."

"I am," said Julie, staring at her monitor.

"I just picked them up, and I can't be certain yet, but they might be heading this way."

Raul turned to Julie and asked, "How long before they get here?"

"Again, at this stage I can't be certain, but my guess would be between twenty and thirty hours," she answered.

"Very well then," said Raul, "I suggest that we do all we can so that we are as ready as we can be."

No one spoke, as they all realized that now, the situation was beyond words.

BATTLE ROYALE

"We are approaching the area, Controller," said Technician Dseto.
"Very well," replied Krerbnot.

"Commandling Ciotglerz, are we ready with the Terra Shaper?" he then asked.

"All is in readiness, Controller," replied the new commandling.

"Maintainer Zeral, are all of our systems functioning as they should?" was Krerbnot's next question.

"We have almost full control," Zeral replied. "There are three minor systems that we are still working on, but that will not affect control of the skyship.

"However," he continued, knowing that what he was about to say, although was not devastating, was not what he would have considered to be an optimal result, "because of the damage we have sustained from the first attack, we will not be able to continuously fire the Razon beam, as this will drain our power supply."

"So, will it still be effective?" asked Krerbnot tersely, thinking that this was information that he should have been told earlier.

"It will still be effective, Controller," replied Zeral optimistically. "It is just that it will have to be fired in short bursts."

"That is good, Maintainer Zeral," said Krerbnot, feeling slightly relieved, before then turning to Dseto and asking, "Technician Dseto, have we located the alien craft yet?"

"We are still scanning, Controller," Dseto replied.

"Very well, then we must know as soon as they are located so that we may attack them before they have time to retaliate," said Krerbnot, knowing that to be defeated was not something that he would accept easily.

"Controller," came an excited call.

"Yes, Technician Dseto?" said Krerbnot in response.

"We have located the alien craft," Dseto replied.

"Navigator Shetklot, take us on a course so as to intercept the craft with haste, so that this time they will be destroyed quickly," said Krerbnot, with a sense of victory in his voice.

"It shall be done, Controller," said Shetklot, as he made sure that the skyship's course was the correct one before gradually increasing speed.

ALONE

As the officers surveyed the crash scene, they both thought that there is no way that anyone could have survived, but still, after they had called for the fire brigade, they had called for paramedics.

As they made their way down the embankment to where the car rested on its roof, they could hear the sirens of the fire truck, wailing in the distance, and knowing that with a clear run it would arrive in about a minute.

When the first officer arrived at the overturned car, he peered inside and said, "There are two bodies."

After he had checked the first and found no signs of life, he checked the second and said, somewhat with amazement, "I've got vitals," letting the other officer know that the second person was still alive, although he was not sure if that was going to be the case for much longer.

"Right, you stay here, and I'll go up and tell the firies we need some cutters," said the second officer, knowing that the fire truck would be equipped with the necessary tools to open up a car like a tin can if needed, and in this case, it would definitely be needed.

Fifteen minutes later, the paramedics were loading the body of the survivor into the ambulance, and they knew that they would have to get to the trauma centre quickly if there were to be any chance of this person making it through the night.

As yet another police car pulled up, the two officers that were first on the scene, noticed it was their duty sergeant that got out of the vehicle, and that he would want a briefing of what happened.

As the two men approached, the sergeant asked, "OK, what happened here?"

"Well," began the first officer, "a call came through about a stolen Stanga Verango, and as I was heading down Fifteenth towards the mini mall, I saw this one go by, and as it fitted the description, I thought I would just do a quick stop and check."

"So I did a U-turn, and as I hit my lights and sirens, it just took off. So that's when I called for back-up," he explained.

The second officer then said, "When I heard the call, I was just coming up on the intersection between Fifteenth and Coffee and I saw them go by, so I assisted in the chase."

"What speeds are we talking about?" asked the sergeant.

"At one stage I hit 195," said the first officer, "and that's when I decided to call it off, as this road gets very difficult very quickly."

"Then it was about a minute later that we came across this."

"Any ID on the occupants?" the sergeant then asked.

"No, but one of them had a personal communication device, and as soon as we can unlock it, we should be able to get some useful numbers out of it," came the answer.

"So, do we know anything about them?" was the sergeant's next question.

"At this stage, only that they both appear to be Caucasians in their mid-teens. The driver would have died on impact, and her passenger probably won't make it to the hospital," replied the officer, giving his sergeant a brief outline of what he saw to be the facts.

The sergeant thought for a few seconds then asked, "What do we know about the car?"

"Reported stolen from a party at a house up at Wilson," was the reply from the first officer.

"OK," the sergeant then said, "I'll need one of you to go to the address and see if all the partygoers can be accounted for, and if they can, then see if anyone was noticed in the area that maybe shouldn't have been there."

"Yeah," said the second officer, "if it's one thing the people at Wilson will do, it's to be able to spot someone that does not fit into their 'socio-economic group' hanging around their area."

"Unfortunately, that is what society has become." replied the sergeant. "The rich feel privileged because of their wealth, and the rest are just poor. But that does not mean that they should be treated any differently when an investigation is taking place and that all courtesies should be extended."

"Anyway," he continued, "get up there and see what you can find."

"And I will need you," he said to the other officer, "to go to the hospital just in case our passenger survives."

"And of course, I will need a full report in the morning," he said, before heading back to his car.

"No worries, Sergeant," they both said, as they too, headed towards their respective patrol cars to carry out their orders, and at the same time realizing, that the paper work for this one, was not going to be minor.

SURVIVAL

"OK," said Julie, "I don't know how close they have to be to fire those sparkly bombs, but I think we should start to turn so—" was as far as she got before she was interrupted by a red beam of light, maybe a metre wide, that flashed past the Moonshaker, just off to the left.

"What was that?" asked Gary.

"I'm not sure, but I think it came from the alien craft," was Julie's reply.

"Great," said Gary, "looks like they found a new toy."

"What do you reckon, Doc? Still be able to stop them?" he then asked.

"All we can do is try, Gary," replied Raul, "but we still have to turn so the impulse gun is pointed at them."

"On it," said Gary, as he started to work the directional controls of the Moonshaker.

"It's getting very close very quickly," said Julie, as yet another beam of light passed them by, this time to the right but farther away than the first.

"Impulse gun is on and charging," said Raul, as they all then saw the massive alien craft pass by approximately five kilometres away.

"Wow, it is very big!" said Dr Peterson in awe at the alien craft's size.

"Yes," replied Raul, "but this was designed to move objects much larger than that."

"They look like they are turning to come back for another go," said Julie, as she watched the huge craft slowly arc its way around.

"OK, just readjusting our turn so that they are in our sights," said Gary, using a term that would have been more common at a shooting range than the position they currently found themselves in.

"So, how are we going with the impulse gun, Doc?" he then asked.

When he got no reply, he turned and said in a questioning tone, "Doc?"

What he saw chilled him to the core, because he noticed Raul staring in Julie's direction. When he looked the same way, he saw Tony standing with his arms around Julie, not allowing her to move, whilst holding a knife to the side of her throat.

"OK, you want to tell me what it is that you think you are doing?" asked Gary in disbelief.

"Don't do anything stupid," said Tony in a threatening tone, as he pressed the knife a little more firmly into Julie's throat.

"No, I think you might have that area covered," replied Gary.

"Always the joker, aren't you?" said Tony savagely, as Gary noticed the knife press even more into Julie's throat.

"Well, not everything can be treated as a joke." Tony added. "Sometimes things get serious, and that might be when people get hurt."

"OK, OK, I was wrong to say that. I'm sorry. So let's calm down and think about this," said Gary trying to put Tony a little more at ease, whilst at the same time knowing that they did not have a great deal of time to waste before the alien craft was going to be able to inflict as much damage upon them as they could.

"I am calm," replied Tony, "and you want to know why—it's because I have faith."

The last statement took Gary a little by surprise.

"I am not sure what faith has to do with it, but if you release Julie and then let us deal with the aliens outside trying their level best to destroy us, I will be glad to have a philosophical conversation with you, once our current situation has been dealt with."

"You just don't get it do you," said Tony.

Gary looked at him quizzically but did not answer, as he had a feeling that Tony was about to try and explain.

He was right, for then Tony went into a ranting tirade that he thought would make them see what he knew.

"I am Tony Watson. God chose me for this mission, because he knew that I would survive no matter what happened, and do you think for a minute, that those godless creatures out there—" he said, extending his arm and pointing the knife in the general direction of the alien craft, which, unfortunately for him, was all the space that Julie needed.

First, she dropped ever so slightly by bending her knees, whilst at the same time shrugging her shoulders.

Then she extended both her arms so as to catch Tony's wrist and keep the knife away from herself before she turned slightly to the right and drove her right elbow back as hard as she could into Tony's stomach at the base of his ribs, causing him to exhale sharply, which would not have been a problem if his bottom rib had not just been broken.

The acute pain he felt caused him to almost black out, and not being able to concentrate, he dropped the knife just as Julie then made a fist of her right hand, punched up as hard as she could so that her bicep was locked tightly under Tony's armpit. At the same time, pulling his right wrist to her left hip, then twisting fiercely to the left, and at the same time extending her right leg slightly to the right and behind, she caused Tony to be flung up and around Julie's hip before crashing with a sickening thud onto the floor.

And as Julie's momentum took her around, she was not totally disappointed to land with her hip into Tony's midriff and hear the popping of another couple of ribs.

When she freed herself from the tangle that she had just created and stood up, she looked at the others staring at her in wide-eyed wonder.

"Classic competition Seoi otoshi," she said in explanation.

Then she added, "All-city open judo champion three years running."

Looking at Tony and realizing that he would be incapacitated for some time, Gary was finally able to once again find his power of speech, and so he asked, "Doc, are we charged up yet?" while still looking at Julie in disbelief.

"We're at 90 per cent," was the reply.

"Here they come again," said Julie, as she was now acting as observer, "and they seem to be taking a direct path to us."

"Red flash, red flash," Julie then said excitedly, "and it's a coming straight for us."

"Doc, now!" shouted Gary, and almost simultaneously, Raul pressed "fire" and "yes" to activate the impulse gun, as the red beam was almost upon them.

ONE MORE TIME

As Kretyabotkl was sitting by Blet's bed, wiping his leathery forehead with a damp cloth, the door opened and Zcetklot entered.

As he walked towards the bed, although he had a smile on his face, it was sadness he felt in his heart to see his Aletal [Dad] lying helpless before him.

"Please," he said, as he placed a hand on Kretyabotkl's shoulder, "I would speak alone."

Knowing her youngling would never be disrespectful towards her, she realized that whatever it was that he had to discuss must be of significance.

"Very well," she said as she rose from her chair, "I will make sure that your meal is being prepared correctly," and she gently squeezed Blet's shoulder and left the room.

When she had gone, Zcetklot looked down at Blet, and was unsure of where to start.

It was Blet that then looked up at his youngling and asked, "What is it that troubles you, my Zlkl [Son]?"

After a short time, Zcetklot said with a sigh, "All my life, I have watched you in awe and with respect, because I knew that the decisions you made were made for the best possible reasons and for the greatest result. Never once did I doubt your ability to make the right choice."

"Your words are kind," said Blet, "but I do not think it is me that you came to speak about."

Zcetklot bowed his head and then said, "I am fearful that I will not be able to make the right decisions, as you do with such ease."

Blet looked up at his youngling and said, "Not all decisions made are going to be the correct ones, even for me."

"But," he continued, "you must never let your fear of being incorrect stop you from trying to decide what you think is best. It is far better to try and fail so that you may learn from your mistakes, than it is to never try and learn nothing."

"But everyone will be looking to me for guidance, and I do not want to let them down," said Zcetklot.

"Once," said Blet, "when I was a youngling of half your age, I wanted so much to impress my Dsetiotb," using the formal term meaning father, "that I pleaded with him to take me on a hunt for glerciad alldo [wild dog]. Their numbers were decreasing, but there was still a small pack roaming in the hills near our village. Finally, he agreed and we would set out early the next morning.

"I remember being woken in what seemed the middle of the night, and I was so tired but I did not want to look as though I was not prepared, so I readied myself as best as I could.

"It was still dark when we set off, and I was already starting to doubt the wisdom of my decision, but I was determined to finish what it was that I had started.

"After walking what seemed an eternity, it started to get light. Then, as we came across a grassy meadow leading to a thicket of brush at the base of a hill, my Dsetiotb stopped, crouched, and said in a whisper, 'We must now be very quiet as the pack has it's lair in that thicket.'

"You will stay behind me with this," he said as he handed me one of the two spears that he was holding.

"It was the Gletb spear [war spear] that his Dsetiotb had won in battle, and I knew it to be an honour.

"As we started slowly through the grassy meadow, crouching and trying not to make any noise, there was a sense of nervous anticipation starting to take hold, and the further into the meadow we went, the greater the tension seemed to be.

"As we were nearing the far edge of the meadow, I was almost bursting with excitement and tension and fear and anticipation, so that when a screeching skrandinki bird took flight just to my right, it gave me such a fright, that I screamed as though my world had just ended.

"Of course, my Dsetiotb immediately turned to see what had happened, and when he saw that I was not in any immediate danger, instead of scolding me for alerting our prey, he just looked at me with a smile and asked if I was all right.

"I felt so ashamed at what I had done I could not help but start to cry.

"My Dsetiotb came to where I stood, kneeled down beside me and said, 'Do not cry, for you have done nothing to shame yourself.'

"'But', I replied, 'it was just a bird and it scared me so.'

"He just looked at me and said, 'What you must do now is remember that sometimes things will happen unexpectedly, and even though it may seem frightening, you must be able to think clearly so that you are able to try and make the correct decisions.'

"'Now, as you can see, the bird is gone, and you are still here unharmed, although I think our pack of glerciad alldo may have heard our approach and be long gone by now. So, let us go home and return another day to rid them from our hills, and you can also think about what happened and what you can do the next time you are frightened.'

"It was in four rotations that we returned, and although the screeching skrandinki birds took flight twice in our journey through the meadow, I did not make a sound, for I was focused on our task and I did not want to be distracted. When we came across the pack of glerciad alldo, we were able to destroy one, and though we only wounded another, the pack fled and did not return.

"So, even though you may be scared, think clearly of your decisions, and trust that what you are doing, you are doing because it is right.

"And remember, everyone has fears, but do not let those fears control you."

Then, looking directly into his youngling's eyes, Blet said, "I know you, and I know this task is one that you are able to perform and perform well."

"Your words give me hope," said Zcetklot, looking down at Blet with a smile starting to form on his face.

"The words I speak are what I see to be the truth," replied Blet, "but you must go now, and show everyone that you are ready to guide them to a better future."

With a new sense of pride welling inside himself Zcetklot said, "I will not let you down."

"Do not let yourself down, and I will never be let down," replied Blet.

Zcetklot gently squeezed Blet's shoulder, before turning to leave so that he may join Krerbnot in the control room and witness the attack on the alien vessel.

As Zcetklot was walking through the living area of their quarters, Kretyabotkl came out of the food preparation area, and said to him, "You know that he sees greatness in you."

"Not as much as I see in him," he replied with a smile before leaving their quarters.

Kretyabotkl watched him leave, with a smile on her face and pride in her heart.

* * *

When Zcetklot arrived at the control room, Krerbnot welcomed him and told him that they had started their attack approach, so the battle would begin shortly.

As he watched, Zcetklot could just make out the alien craft in the distance.

"Controller, enemy craft within range," said Technician Dseto.

Krerbnot turned to Ciotglerz and said, "Commandling, fire when ready."

Ciotglerz gave the command, and almost immediately the Razon beam streaked its way towards the Moonshaker.

"Attack unsuccessful," said Dseto.

"Beam has missed its target," she added.

"Adjust and refire," said Ciotglerz.

The skyship altered course slightly, and another red beam burst forth from the Terra Shaper.

This time they were close enough so that everyone could see that the beam had missed its target.

As they went past the strange craft, Technician Dseto said, "Controller, the alien craft does not appear to be moving."

"Can you explain, Technician Dseto?" Krerbnot asked.

"During our first attack, the craft was trying to move out of the way before it turned to try and escape. Now, it is not moving at all," she said.

"Could it be that it was somehow damaged in the first attack?" asked Zcetklot.

"That could be so, Overbeing," said Krerbnot, "but still, we must take no chances."

"Controller," said Commandling Ciotglerz, "if we can attack from below this craft, and it does try to flee the battle, it will do so in a straight line, so that we will not have to alter our angle of attack, and therefore, greatly increase our chances of success."

"Very good," said Krerbnot, before adding, "Navigator Shetklot, bring us to a course so that we may be in direct line below the enemy craft."

"Yes, Controller," answered Shetklot.

As the skyship slowly turned until it was in direct line below the Moonshaker, Krerbnot told Ciotglerz to wait until he gave the order to fire, as he wanted to get as close as possible so that they would be sure of a direct hit and certain victory.

As they got closer and closer, although they would not show it, everyone watching was becoming more anxious, and they began to think that surely they were close enough, but still Krerbnot did not give the order to fire.

"Ready, ready," said Krerbnot, as even he was starting to think that maybe he had pushed further than he should.

"FIRE!" he then said in a loud and stern voice.

Once again, almost immediately after Ciotglerz had relayed the order, a red beam snaked its way towards the Moonshaker.

Everyone watched in anticipation, as the beam seemed to be heading in a direct path towards its target.

SPECTACLE

If there had been anyone on Earth at the time and the sky had been clear, they would have been able to stare at the bright red flash that had occurred in the night sky with wonder at its brilliance, but as it was, there was no one there, and so it went almost unnoticed.

The occupants of the opaque craft who had been watching proceedings from a distance began to discuss what they had just witnessed.

These strange beings, although they had solid form, were almost translucent, and to communicate with each other they had long since abandoned the use of vocalizing and relied now on communal thoughts, so that everyone would know what was meant when something was being discussed.

"It would appear that one craft has been destroyed," was the first thought of the being who was watching closely the battle that was playing out before them.

"Yes," came another thought, "it would seem that the inhabitants of this sector are still barbaric in their dealings with each other."

"We must return to central and inform them of what we have witnessed, and to also inform them of the damage done to this world."

"Indeed," seemed to be the general consensus.

And so the craft turned before almost immediately disappearing in a bright flash that sped them on their way home.

FINAL GOODBYES

As Ray Stevens sat at the bank of monitors that had not been used since that fateful day he placed the paper bag that he had brought in on the desk in front of himself, and from it he produced the bottle of whiskey and two glasses.

As he was opening the bottle, he turned at a noise that he heard from behind.

It was Steve.

"Do you always use two glasses when you drink alone?" Steve asked with a smile.

"Sorry," replied Ray, "I did not think anyone else would be here."

"It's all right," said Steve, "your secret's safe with me."

"No, I was just going to have a last drink with the crew of the mission, before heading off to the memorial," Ray explained.

"Yeah, I think I just wanted to come in and say my last goodbyes as well," said Steve.

Then he asked, "Do you think they would mind if I shared in your toast?"

"I don't see why they would," said Ray as he filled both glasses and handed one to Steve.

He then raised his glass and said, "Here's to the crew. May their bravery be an example to us all."

Steve answered with, "Hear, hear," before they both emptied their respective glasses in one shot.

"Whoo, man alive," said Steve, "that's kinda potent."

"Yes," replied Ray, "it was what Gary would sometimes bring in if we worked very late."

"Does it get any smoother?" Steve asked, wondering why anyone would want more than one drink.

"Actually, after about three or four, it starts to lose its edge," said Ray, as he once again filled both glasses.

"I don't think I will try and find out if you are right today," said Steve, "because I do not want to get to the service smashed, which is what I think three or four of these will do."

He then took a small sip and thought that it was not quite as bad as the initial shock from the first gulp.

"So, they're starting up again next week," he then said.

"Yeah," said Ray, "and from what I can gather, security is going to be through the roof."

"I thought it was last time," said Steve, "until Graham Strand decided to show his hand."

"Yes, it's amazing what greed can do to people," Ray replied, before adding, "and although he will be in prison a long time, it will not bring Dr Western and the others back."

Both of them contemplated what had just been said for a few moments before Steve next spoke.

"Well, I guess we better get going if we want to get there before the service starts," and he finished his drink in one gulp.

He grimaced and said, "I think it might take more than three or four of these, before it starts to get smooth."

Ray swallowed his drink and replied, "Oooh, I think you might be right."

Then, looking at the microphone extending from the desk towards him, Ray leaned forward, activated it and said, "Moonshaker one, this is Mission Control, can you hear me? Over."

After a few moments of silence, he then said, "Moonshaker one, wherever you are guys, I hope it is a better place," before sitting back in his seat.

Steve placed a comforting hand on Ray's shoulder before saying, "Come on, we better get going."

"You're right," replied Ray, "let's get out of here," as they then both made to get up and head to the memorial, whilst at the same time knowing, that although they would do their jobs as best as they could on the new project, it did not mean that it was going to be easy.

OLD FRIENDS

After the flash had subsided and their craft had steadied, they all looked around, first at each other to make sure they were all well and then they started to scour the skies for any sign of the alien craft.

"Are you able to see them?" asked Raul.

"Not out this side," said Julie.

"They're not out here either," said Gary.

"But we have been pushed towards the Moon," he said excitedly, as they all turned and noticed how close they were.

"Gary," said Raul with more than a little urgency, "turn us so we can propel ourselves away before we get too close."

"On it, Doc," replied Gary as they then noticed the massive dust cloud erupt from the surface of the Moon at the same time as it appeared to give an ever so slight shiver.

"Look at that," said Ashley.

"Yes, impressive," said Raul before asking, "Are we moving away yet, Gary?"

"Getting there, Doc," came Gary's reply.

"We have to get away from here before we get too close and the Moon's gravity grabs us," said Raul, trying to convey the urgency of their situation.

"Doc," said Gary, "can you fire the impulse gun at the Moon and maybe give us a little boost?"

"Worth a try," said Raul, as he noticed the power setting on the impulse gun had already reached 72 per cent.

As the satellite rotated so that it was now facing directly away from the Moon, Gary had the directional thrusters operating at a level that he knew was going to give him maximum effect without overusing the power supply.

Raul, knowing that he could wait no more, fired the impulse gun, then watched, as yet another dust cloud erupted from the surface of the Moon that intermingled with the first and began billowing into space.

After a few seconds, Gary said in a jubilant tone, "I think that did it, Doc."

"Good," replied Raul.

"Now, can we see the other craft anywhere?" he then asked.

'I did not see them go anywhere," said Julie, "and I can't find them on any scan I've done."

"Do you think we have destroyed them?" asked Ashley.

"We have yet to see," said Raul trying not to get overenthusiastic about it.

Hearing a slight moan, Gary turned to look at Tony lying on the floor holding his ribs, and asked, "What are we going to do with him?"

Raul also turned, and said, "I am not really—"

"Moonshaker One, this is Mission Control, can you hear me? Over."

Everybody froze, not willing to ask each other if they had also heard what was just said in case the answer was no.

Still stunned into inaction, Raul was staring at the intercom when it came to life once more.

"Moonshaker One, wherever you are guys, I hope it is a better place."

Raul then almost stumbled in his attempt to reach the intercom, but eventually was able to reach it and reply, "Mission control, this is Moonshaker One. Can you hear us?"

FINAL FAIRWELLS

"Are you able to locate the alien craft?" asked Krerbnot.

"We have done many scans, Controller, and we are unable to locate them anywhere," replied Technician Dseto.

"Could it be that they were destroyed in the battle?" asked Zcetklot.

"That is our hope," said Krerbnot, "but to make sure, we must check to see that they have not just been able to flee somehow and be waiting nearby to attack us when we are not expecting it."

"Controller, I have just located an energy reading from the edge of our sector," said Dseto.

"What is the source of this reading?" asked Krerbnot of his technician.

"It would appear that another craft has just departed the area," answered Dseto.

"Why were we not able to locate it earlier?" asked Krerbnot.

"It was in an area many reels distance and there was not the need to scan so far away," Dseto explained, hopefully to the satisfaction of the controller.

Commandling Ciotglerz then said, "Could it be, that the distant craft was from the same world as the alien vessel we have just destroyed, and that seeing that destruction, they have returned to their home world?"

After thinking for a few seconds, Krerbnot said, "You may be right, Commandling, but we must still search to make sure that they are gone."

And so they searched, and when Dseto finally said, "Controller, we have scanned the whole sector and there is no sign of the alien ship at all." Krerbnot at last started to relax.

"Very well," he said, before adding, "Technician Dseto, keep a vigil in case it is a trick, and Maintainer Zeral, you will check the skyship for any damage. Well done to you and Commandling Ciotglerz in your efforts in destroying the alien vessel."

"It is an honour to be of service," replied Zeral, beaming with pride.

"Now, Overbeing Zcetklot," Krerbnot then said as he turned to face him, "if I could ask you to inform the sayers of our current situation, and I will organize the departing ceremony for our citizens that were sent to the Great Protector by our enemy, as well as inform everyone else of what has happened."

"It shall be done, Controller," replied Zcetklot, as he realized that this would be his first official duty as overbeing, and even though he thought of it as an honour, he also hoped that he would not have to attend to too many. He wanted his Aletal to continue his duties as soon as he was well enough, and with some luck, that would be soon.

*   *   *

It was in two rotations time wise that they had all gathered in the large meeting hall to farewell the twenty-eight citizens who had been taken from them.

Healer Retkrotz sat with a forlorn look on his face, thinking of what he may have been able to do extra that could have saved the three injured citizens that were taken, and even though, deep down, he knew that he had done all that he could, it still did not ease the pain of loss.

Kretyabotkl and Etklet sat in the first row, looking at the drape covered body of Blet, who was to be the first to be sent to the new world below.

Kretyabotkl was looking at the shrouded body of her sharebeing, and remembered the day of their Rlerklerkldo Shotbotkrlklo [joining ceremony], and thought with a smile, how she looked at him and thought that he was so handsome that everyone else may as well have been covered in mud, for they would never look as good as he did that day or ever would on any other day.

She was saddened beyond words by her loss, but she also knew that others were grieving and that the time she had shared with him would be something she could never lose.

When all the speeches had been made and all the tributes had been paid, Controller Krerbnot gave the command, and slowly, one by one, the bodies were relayed down to the ejection area and they were then committed to their new home that of the dust-covered world below.

*   *   *

After the ceremony, Krerbnot held a meeting to decide on their next course of action.

During these discussions, it was decided that the best thing to do, because of the damage to the skyship and the state of the new world, would be to return to Yendor, so that they may be able to carry out the repairs needed, as well as inform everyone of what has happened.

Then, they would be able to set off on a journey to one of the new worlds that their knowledge seekers had found before they had left.

And so, after all citizens had been informed, they set out for the skyhole and their path home.

WELCOME HOME

Three days later, as the shuttle that had been sent to retrieve the lost crew touched down, the crowd of onlookers burst into cheers of joy, as well as many of the millions of viewers watching the news broadcast all around the world.

One of the news reporters doing a live cross to the landing site spoke into the camera in response from his anchor man in the studio.

"Well, Jim, as you can see, and no doubt hear, the scenes of jubilation here at the landing site are unparalleled. The people here are just yelling and cheering and clapping and hugging total strangers, such is the mood here. It is just totally amazing."

"That's true, Roger," replied the studio anchor, "it does look amazing, but not quite as amazing as some of the stories that we are hearing of the exploits of the crew."

"I mean, if what is being said is true—time travel, alien attacks—it's just so hard to comprehend."

"You're right, Jim. I guess we will just have to wait for the crew to tell us what actually happened whilst they were on their journey."

"But now," said the reporter as he turned to look to where the shuttle had come to a rest, "you can see the shuttle being surrounded by vehicles. There are fire trucks and ambulances and about four or five black vans."

"Maybe they are scared that they might disappear again," said the studio anchor with a chuckle.

"You might be right, Jim, but I don't think they will get the chance now, as we see the door in the side of the shuttle open, and the stairs being backed into position so everyone can get out."

It was a few tense seconds later before Roger spoke again, but when he did, it was almost an excited shout, as he too, was being caught up in the moment.

"Yes, yes, we can see the first of the crew members coming out of the door, and it looks to be Dr Raul Western, the man behind this project, standing and waving to the crowd, who I might add, are almost in a frenzy at this moment.

"As he looks around, we can see his wife, Tania, standing there with tears of joy streaming down her face, as she looks at her husband slowly descending the stairs, before she rushes forward to embrace him.

"Next we see Gary Roebottom leaving the shuttle, as we might try to make our way over to see if we can get a word with Dr Western," said Roger, as he then started to head towards the police cordon, to see if he might be able to get Dr Western's attention.

As he was heading over, Roger noticed that someone that appeared to be an official, went to Dr Western and his wife, and said something that seemed to shock them both, as Tania then started to cry almost uncontrollably, and Dr Western, just stared ahead blankly as the colour seemed to fade from his face before they were then bundled into one of the waiting vans and driven away.

On the trip into the city, not too many words were exchanged as Tania tried to control her emotions as best as she could, whilst Raul did all he could to comfort her.

When they arrived at their destination, they were led down several corridors before finally arriving at a room that they were told could have the body of their daughter in it.

When they had assured the doctor that they were ready to go in, the door was opened, and Tania thought her heart would break looking at Ellie lying there, motionless, with so many tubes in her, and so many machines hooked up to her, she could not bear to think of how much she must be hurt.

The doctor explained that she had been brought in a few days ago, and although they were doing all they could for her, it was up to Ellie to fight for her own survival.

Raul looked at his daughter lying motionless on the bed, feeling responsible for everything that would ever happen to her, and said, "Oh, Ellie, what have I done? I should never have left."

Tania looked up at Raul and said, "It is not your fault. I am the one that should have been looking out for her."

"OK, folks, do not blame yourselves," said the Doctor, "the fact is, that your daughter is still alive, and when she wakes up, she is going to need support from both of you."

Raul looked at the doctor and nodded in agreement before asking, "Of course, Doctor, what is it we can do?"

"Well," replied the Doctor, "in a situation such as this, although they cannot respond, in most circumstances the patient can actually hear what is being said."

"So if you want to speak to her and give her a little positive reinforcement," continued the Doctor, "that could be a good start."

Raul once again nodded to the Doctor, then turned back to look at Ellie and just stood there unsure of what to say.

After standing there for a few silent moments not knowing where to start, he finally said, "Oh, Sweetie, what have you done to yourself? You know that if ever you want to talk to us, we will always listen, and who knows, I might even learn to put up with Terry."

This last statement caused Tania to laugh through her tears, and she hugged her husband tighter as she rested her head on his chest.

"Ellie," continued Raul as he gently squeezed his daughter's hand, "I will never leave you again."

"Promise?" came the croaky response from Ellie as she struggled to open her eyes.

As Tania gasped, then covered her face with her hands and once more burst into tears, although this time they were tears of elation, Raul just gently touched the ends of Ellie's fingers and said, "Butterfly promise."

THE RETURNING

As the skyhole started to appear in the distance, Krerbnot could not help but notice the change in its configuration.

For no longer was there a defined circle at the entrance, but what appeared to be an ever-changing oval shape rotating and contorting in different directions.

Krerbnot consulted with his technicians, starguides, maintainers, and knowledge seekers, and although it was not without risk, it was the general consensus, that it would be safe to travel through.

That, with the fact that the skyship needed repair and they could not stay on the new world, meant that Krerbnot could see that he did not really have any options other than to proceed.

As they approached the skyhole, Krerbnot could see just how much of a difference there was from the first time they had entered.

No longer was there a defined edge, but a general haze extending inwards and outwards, so that the entrance was approximately half of the size it was before.

"Entering the skyhole," said Technician Dseto.

Expecting to see the magnificent light show that usually accompanied vessels that journey into the skyhole, Krerbnot was quite taken aback to see that the brilliant colours were somewhat lessened and that there seemed to be more of a dark haze that was spread throughout.

Also, if you were to look closely, you could see stars in the distance, through the side of the skyhole, as they were travelling through.

But, Krerbnot thought, all had said that the journey could be made, and it would not be too long before they were safe, for the time being, back on Yendor.

It was five rotations time wise later that Technician Dseto had voiced her concerns to Krerbnot about changes she had been noticing in the skyhole and the effect those changes were having on the skyship.

Once again Krerbnot summoned his key personnel to a meeting to discuss their current situation and options.

During these discussions it was decided that they could not stay in the skyhole, for if it were to collapse with them in it, it could cause massive damage to the ship. They could not just exit through the side.

Because of the rotating nature of the skyhole the damage caused would be catastrophic.

Maintainer Zeral suggested that, if the walls of the skyhole were somehow weakened before they exited, the skyship would have a greater chance of survival.

"How would it be possible for this to be done?" asked Krerbnot.

"Now," said Zeral as he started to explain, "the walls of the skyhole are not solid or stable enough to allow our weapons to explode on impact, and if we could time it so that they exploded close enough to disrupt the wall, it would still not create a gap large enough or stay open long enough, for us to pass through."

"But," he continued, "if we were to turn the skyship towards where the weapons were headed and then fire the Razon beam at them when they were just about to contact the wall, it would increase the power of the blast greatly, and this should create a hole large enough that would stay open long enough for us to pass through."

Krerbnot then asked his knowledge seekers, if the nature of the skyhole was such, that Zeral's idea had merit.

All agreed that Zeral's idea was one that could very well work.

Once again, knowing that they had limited options, it was agreed that Zeral's plan was to be put into action.

When the agreed upon time came around, Krerbnot made sure that everyone was ready, before he then gave the order to launch the weapons.

As the weapons got closer and closer to the side of the skyhole, Krerbnot then gave the order to turn the skyship and fire the Razon beam, then head towards the bright flash caused by the explosion.

The ship exited in one piece through the side of the skyhole but not before being severely buffeted and thrown about as though it were a youngling's plaything.

Krerbnot immediately asked for a report on any damages that they may have sustained.

The reply he got, did not fill him with confidence.

"Controller," said Zeral, "I am getting reports from the rear of the skyship of extreme structural damage. Everything is still intact, but it has been severely weakened."

Then Shetklot said, "Yes, I think this is so, for I am having much difficulty in being able to navigate with any accuracy, and I fear that I may lose control altogether before too long."

"Starguide Stbetsho, do we know how far from Yendor we are?" Krerbnot asked.

"That is not an answer I can give, Controller, for we are beyond the edge of the great unknown," replied Stbetsho.

Krerbnot knew that this was not an ideal situation, but he also remembered something he was told as a youngling that stuck in his mind, and that was that where there was life, there was hope.

"Starguide Stbetsho, can you scan the area with Technician Dseto to see if you are able to locate a world close enough for us to get to."

"Of course, Controller," Stbetsho replied.

"Maintainer Zeral," he then said, "you must proceed to the damaged area and see what can be done."

"I am on my way, Controller," said Zeral as he headed out of the control room.

"Overbeing Zcetklot," Krerbnot then said, "if you could work with Commandling Ciotglerz in making sure that everyone is able to access the escape shuttles if the need arises, that would be of great assistance."

"And I will inform every one of what is occurring and what it is that may have to be done," he concluded, more to himself than anyone in particular.

It was after Krerbnot had made the announcement to all the citizens on the skyship about what was happening and after Zeral had informed him that the skyship could not be repaired, that Starguide Stbetsho said a little excitedly, "Controller, I think we may have found a suitable world."

"Is it far?" Krerbnot asked.

Technician Dseto answered.

"At our current speed, it will take two rotations time wise to reach it."

After he had consulted with Zeral, and had been told that the skyship would possibly not be able to complete the journey, Krerbnot advised all citizens, that they must start preparations for an evacuation, and be sure to know which of the escape shuttles that they were allocated to.

It was almost two rotations time wise later, that, acting on information received from Zeral, Krerbnot actually gave the command to board the escape shuttles, and because Maintainer Zeral and his team were able to keep the skyship in one piece as well as still being able to travel, almost all of what would be needed to start a new life on the strange new world they were about to inhabit, was able to be loaded for evacuation.

Standing in the control room watching the shuttles start to depart, Krerbnot began to wonder what the future may hold for them.

And although he knew this was not the world they had set out for, it was someplace where he was sure that they would be able to survive.

Eventually it was Navigator Shetklot who broke his train of thought when he said, "Controller, it will be soon that I have no control over the skyship."

"Very well," Krerbnot replied, as he then turned to Dseto and asked.

"How many shuttles are left to depart?"

The answer came, "They have almost all departed, and they are ready with one last one for our departure."

Krerbnot took one long last look around the control room, before saying to the few crew members that had remained behind, "You have all done well, but now it is time for us to leave."

All that remained to do before they left were the final tasks that certain individuals knew they had to carry out.

Shetklot shut down the drive engines but kept the stabilizing thrusters operating so that the shuttle that they took would not be struck by the skyship twisting and spiralling out of control.

Dseto made sure to send one last message, in the hope that one day it would be picked up and their new world would be found.

When the last of the citizens were loaded into the final three shuttles, Krerbnot could not help but feel a little saddened by the fact that this once mighty skyship would be left to wander aimlessly throughout the vast expanse of the void that was the great unknown.

When the shuttle left the skyship, they all looked back at the slowly spiralling ship and could finally see the extent of the damage caused by exiting the skyhole, and all were amazed at the ability of Zeral and his team to be able to keep it functioning as it did.

With a sigh, Krerbnot turned to see the long line of shuttles advancing towards their new home in the distance, and then said, "A new world, a new beginning, and this is where our lives must start."

The others said nothing, as they were contemplating what it was that the future held in store for them all.

And the shuttle continued, silently heading towards their final destination.

SILVER LINING

Three years, four months, and two days later.

"Welcome back to our coverage of this, the forty-fifth Olympic Games, coming to you live from Alice Springs, here in the heart, or as they say here, 'the red centre', of Australia.

"Ever since the discovery of the largest deposit of Palentium on Earth, Alice Springs has become one of the most important and fastest growing cities in Australia, and with a population of just over two million people, it is by no means the smallest.

"Also, the wealth being generated by royalties paid to the indigenous peoples of this area, has seen the advent of more than one extremely successful business venture.

"Right now, we are going to cross to the Araluen sporting complex that has been built with thanks to the generous sponsorship of one of those ventures, the Central Indigenous Mining Corporation, and it is truly a remarkable complex.

"Are you there Grant?"

"I'm here, thanks, Kevin," came the reply from the reporter at the complex, "and I am with local reporter, and some would say, fitness legend, Lorraine Butterworth."

"Thanks, Grant, it's good to be here," replied Lorraine.

"You know, you are right when you say this is a remarkable complex Kevin," said Grant. "The fact is, that although we have been here a week, I am still totally amazed at this incredible structure.

"I mean, to use photoelectric glass so that not only can you look out at the 360-degree uninterrupted view, you are able to create your own energy at the same time, it's actually brilliant in its simplicity," said Grant enthusiastically.

"Whoa, someone once told me that judo players did not use big words," said Kevin light-heartedly goading his colleague, "and you have just used three or four. What's going on?"

"Yes," replied Grant. "I actually got to go to a training session last night, and I think I may have been thrown a bit too hard and something got loosened up."

"OK," said Kevin with a smile and a slight laugh, "you better tell us what is happening."

"Thanks, Kevin," Grant then said. "We are just waiting for the final of the women's open between Ellie Western and the Iranian girl, Tashmire Fenare."

"It is just remarkable to think how far Ellie has come in the last three years since that horrific car accident she was involved in."

"Yes," said Lorraine, "it just shows the dedication and hard work she has put in to get here has paid off."

"There she is now, talking to her coach, who is another one with an incredible story," said Grant.

"Yes, indeed, who does not know the name of Julie Anders?" Lorraine asked rhetorically.

"Soon to be Julie Roebottom," Grant quickly added.

"Yes," mused Lorraine, "how could you compete with the stories that they will be able to tell their grandchildren?"

Grant burst into laughter at Lorraine's last statement.

Lorraine just looked at him with a wonderful smile on her face.

When he was able to control himself, Grant said, "Yes, I suppose it would be more interesting talking about when you went back in time, fought aliens, then came back and put the Moon back into its orbit, rather than the time I went surfing with my uncle and stood on a starfish."

"But now," he continued, after he had been able to control himself, "as you can see, the contestants have just been called, so they are making their way to the mat, then bowing at the edge before proceeding to the centre, bowing again, and waiting for the referee to begin the bout."

When he had made sure that both contestants and all officials were ready, the referee called in a loud voice, "Hajime!" signifying the start of the fight.

Cautiously, the two contestants circled the mat, looking for a chance to grapple, or get a controlling grip on the others judogi.

It was Ellie who tried first to get a hold of the lapel of the Iranian girl, and for a few seconds, it was as though two cats were pawing at each other, for one would reach and the other would push her hand away, not once, but several times very rapidly.

"Ellie, get your grip, get your grip!" Julie was yelling at her.

Tashmire was more cautious and was moving sideways, trying to grip Ellie's sleeve.

As Tashmire took hold of the sleeve, Ellie was able to grab the Iranian girl's lapel and immediately tried a side-foot sweep.

Julie excitedly yelled, "Yes," when she thought that Ellie had been successful, but although she stumbled slightly, Tashmire was able to regain her footing.

It was as the Iranian girl was regaining her footing, that Ellie was then able to grab hold of her right sleeve, and attempt a shoulder technique.

But as she did not bring her left leg back, much to the annoyance of Julie who was yelling at her to get all the way in, she could not complete the throw, and when she attempted to turn back out, Tashmire then straightened her left leg and placed it behind Ellie and dropped to the mat whilst pulling Ellie down, forcing her to stumble then fall flat on her back, and the referee had no hesitation in raising his arm and calling "Ippon."

Julie turned and threw her hands into the air in frustration before then applauding both girls, Tashmire for winning the fight and Ellie for making the gold medal fight at the Olympics.

After getting a hug from her opponent, Ellie congratulated her, and then bowed again before leaving the mat and heading to Julie, who did her best to console her as the tears started to flow.

Julie reminded her, that she had just fought for gold at the Olympic Games, and that currently, she was the second best female judo player in the world, which is something that she should be proud of and that with an uninterrupted training schedule, she would have her revenge at the grand prix meet in six months' time.

Then she pointed out Raul, Tania, and Gary, sitting in the second row still smiling and clapping. Seeing her looking their way, they all waved, and it seemed that if their smiles got any larger, their jaws would surely fall off.

It was at the awards ceremony that Ellie finally started to grasp what it was that she had achieved, and after the bronze medals had been awarded, her name was called.

Climbing the dais, as proud as she felt with her parent's friends and team mates watching and cheering, Ellie knew that this is what she wanted, and that she still had one more step to climb.

After she had been presented with her medal, and Tashmire's name was called, the scene started to pull back, so that we see the complex, then we see it on the outskirts of town.

Then it pulls back farther, so that we can see the outline of Australia, then the world in its entirety.

As it gets smaller, we see the Moon, before it too starts to fade into the distance, before finally we see the edge of what appears to be a vast space craft, hanging silently in space.

Rotation—Day—28 hours
Cycle—Year—430 days
Mid time—Noon
IMPol—Investigative branch of the military police
Krel—Unit of measure, 1.2 metres
Mitnar—1000 Krels
Reel—1000 Krels
Span—1000 Reels
Aletal—Dad
Zlkl—Son
Glerciad Alldo—Wild dog
Gletb—War
R l e r k l e r k l d o Shotbotkrlklo—Joining ceremony
A—ET
B—N
C—SH
D—AL
E—OT
F—DS
G—DO
H—C
I—ER
J—R
K—BN
L—CI
M—KR
N—KL
O—L
P—F
Q—DR
R—B
S—Z
T—ST
U—YA
V—TR

W—GL
X—KOI
Y—O
Z—YE
CH—F
TH—I
SH—X
PH—J
WH—M